From Unicorns To Wild Geese

sequel to the Blackberry Pickers

With love
& Best Wishes

Lorrie James

From Unicorns To Wild Geese

sequel to the Blackberry Pickers

Louise James

AuthorHouse™ UK
1663 Liberty Drive
Bloomington, IN 47403 USA
www.authorhouse.co.uk
Phone: 0800.197.4150

Published by AuthorHouse 12/17/2014

ISBN: 978-1-4969-9691-6 (sc)
ISBN: 978-1-4969-9692-3 (e)

This book is dedicated to my late parents
Reginald Thomas and Violet Louise Underhill
I still miss you

Acknowledgements

I wish to thank all the team at AuthorHouse for making dreams come true. Thanks to Cherri Gibson and her team of coordinators and Thank you to the graphics team for taking my humble illustrations and using them for the cover of my books.

I am very grateful for all your constant help and advice. Thank you.

Chapter 1

The last rays of sunset glowed through the trees, glimpses of gold and violet rose stretched across the sky briefly lighting the clearing with pale light. The first stars were appearing from an indigo backcloth while a chill wind murmured through the forest. Somewhere a waking owl tried a tentative "Woo" as the shadows deepened. There came a rustling as some night creature moved through the undergrowth but the watching man never stirred his eyes fast on the disappearing sun.

He stood hunched as someone old might stand the cool breeze ruffling his hair. He was motionless until the last flock of colour left the sky and all around was dark only then he sighed and turned towards the cottage which nestled in the clearing behind him. It loomed dark and silent. He could just make out the boarded windows and the door buried beneath creepers.

A wry smile twisted his lip as he remembered moving boards to gain access to this same cottage years ago. He would enter the same way tonight. He stood a little longer as if waiting for someone or something until a pale moon lit the scene gently touching everything to silver. The cottage took on a magical quality, enchanted; its neglected state flattered by moonlight. The man moved at last towards the broken gate set in the low wall that surrounded what had once been a garden. He swung it a few times as if testing its sturdiness. It finally came to rest sagging drunkenly against its post.

He walked the path slowly as someone waking from a long sleep until he reached the door where he had to trample the briars that barred his way. As before a loose board gave way under pressure and he soon removed the others only to find the door behind them locked. He paused a moment smiling then crossed the clearing to where a tumbledown shed had once housed a goat. The door was gone but he slid his hand high above the lintel until his fingers found a long flat tin, he shook it, his cache had remained safe; inside a key to the cottage and a penknife which had belonged to an old pedlar he had once known. He slipped it into his pocket where it clinked satisfyingly against his army knife. As he returned to the cottage he heard a rustle, as he turned, a deer bounded past then stopped under the tress to look at him. The stag appeared almost white in the moonlight. He gasped for it appeared to only have one horn. He stood rigid for a moment not believing what he was seeing. Then the stag bounded away into the forest. He mentally shook himself, there were a lot of deer in these woods and one could have easily lost an antler or only grown one? He turned again to the cottage shaking his head at his fancies.

A sharp click and he was inside. The never forgotten smell of soot and mice hit him like a blow from the past. He hesitated for a moment as if afraid to enter. Other smells seemed to hang ghostlike in the air, fresh bread and rabbit stew, paraffin, blackberry jam and soap. He remembered how Janet his older sister liked to scrub the table and floor. He could almost hear his sister Amy's shrill complaining voice and Janet's lower soothing tones. Tears suddenly filled his throat, the lit match burning his fingers; he dropped it swearing and lit another.

Furniture was piled in the centre of the room with the big turkey red carpet (he remembered it coming from the Hall) thrown over it. Moving further into the room he noticed a lantern hanging from a beam. He took it down and shook it wondering as it still containing paraffin, gently he raised the glass and lit the wick a soft warm glow filled the room.

He moved to the range where again he was surprised to find paper and kindling to hand and a basket of logs nearby. Someone must have meant to return and didn't, dust lay thick over everything. It couldn't have been here since Amy and Sep left. His mind went blank, he must not think about people – it wasn't safe.

He busied himself with the fire and the room soon warmed. He remembered the first time he lit this old range, the chimney had gone on fire but it seemed alright now, the fire burned clear and bright. He hesitated to look in the boxes, they would keep. On second thoughts he rummaged until he found a kettle, frying pan, mug and plate. These were the same boxes his sister had packed when she left nothing had changed only him he thought as he walked back across the clearing. He found the little waterfall he remembered, still tumbling into an old trough, holding the kettle under the running water he reasoned it should be alright, he had drunk it many times in the past and much worse since.

Boiling the kettle he opened the bag he had carried and made tea (no sugar or milk he hadn't had those for a long time), toasting the bread and cheese he brought with him, he realized he would have to venture out to buy food, dreading the thought realizing he had no choice. Surely no one would recognize him blond hair streaked with grey and he had a beard which he hated and would get rid of at the first opportunity. He couldn't remember his age. Unrolling the carpet he laid it double in front of the fire, removing his boots and wrapping himself in his greatcoat he fell instantly asleep. When deep in the night dreadful noises came from the cottage, only the owl was listening. Calls, incoherent shouts and screams filled the night culminating in heart breaking sobs.

The owl flew away.

Something scrabbling on the roof woke the new tenant and he lay for a while wondering where he was, starting up in sudden panic then remembering where he was, he released a sigh and relaxed. Birdsong filtered through the badly fitting windows and he found himself listening with awe to the first dawn chorus he'd heard since his teens. April in England, the woods would be full of windflowers and bluebells, primroses and violets always bloomed under the garden wall. The sap would be rising giving the trees that wonderful coat of green which would deepen every day until they were in full leaf. With a sudden rush of excitement he rose and flung open the door. The volume of birdsong sent him reeling. He had forgotten the sheer beauty of a dawn chorus. Every bird in the forest was in full song, their voices drawing the life force from roots deep in the earth up to the trees and plants unfolding buds. From the horrors of the night came the glory of the dawn.

He flung off his clothes running to plunge his face and arms into the stone trough, scrubbing his body with leaves and the fine sand which lay in the bottom, it stung and burned. "I'm clean, clean, clean. He yelled into the trees. Running back to the cottage he dried himself in front of the fire. His clothes smelt of the hospital disinfectant but until he could buy some more he was stuck with them; rubbing a hand over his face, he vowed again to rid himself of his beard for although the hospital had cleaned him up he could still feel the lice that had crept over him, he shuddered.

He carried the boxes and furniture outside and laid the carpet over the stone floor, although old and slightly worn in places it fitted the room and looked good. He only hoped the old agreement was still in place that anyone in need could live in the cottage rent free. Placing the table and chairs to his satisfaction and the two armchairs either side of the fire, the sideboard fitting against the wall where he knew it had stood before, he then carried the chest into the bedroom before returning to open the boxes, as he thought; they were untouched since Amy had left, then he remembered that Sep's mother had died and let them her house, they would have had all they needed. China, saucepans, books, cushions and towels were all here with bedding, blankets and rugs all of which had been sent from Arlington Hall when the Penry's lived here. Realizing there was no mattress on the iron bed frame in the other room, he was glad of the rugs and blankets, with his greatcoat he would be warm enough.

Food was the next thing in his mind he didn't want to go to the village as he might run into Amy who lived there with her husband Sep and their children or anyone else who might recognise him. He remembered a cart used to pick them up to go to the market in St Austell's maybe there was a bus now or he would walk, safer that way. He had his gratuity so he had money for a while; he vaguely remembered having a bank book but couldn't remember where it might be or what was in it.

It took but a minuet to close the windows and lock the door, crossing the wood passing the ruined cottages and mill which looked no worse in their dereliction than they did before he left. Following the stream which ran into a small lake, he lay for a while on the bank and waited; an hour or so later he was back at the cottage and two fat trout were sizzling in the pan. He hadn't lost the old art of tickling.

After the meal he slipped into a doze, he was always tired. Startled awake he heard voices coming up the path. He wasn't quick enough to rise and lock the door, a voice he recognised called out.

He rose quickly cursing. He should have been prepared for this to happen when he came here. Joe Treggorran was coming to the door followed by a red haired young man who could only be his son. At the doorway Joe stopped in his tracks then his bright blue eyes alight he rushed forwards hand outstretched. "Tis' Tom, as I live, Tom Penry?" Joe sensed a withdrawal as the man stepped back and he hesitated. "Sorry you have the wrong man. My name is Jack Travers. Perhaps I shouldn't be here but I was told it would be alright by someone in the village."

Joe stood silent eyeing the man up and down. True this man was taller than he remembered, much broader. His fair hair straight and streaked with grey, looked weary and older than he should be but he had the cornflower blue eyes and the merry smile of the boy he remembered, eyes he would know anywhere and didn't his sister Amy have the same?

He started forwards again. "Come on Tom, you be 'having us on. You grew up with us. I'd know ee anywhere."

"I tell you I am not Tom whoever he may be. My name is Jack Travers and I need a place to stop for a bit." He faltered under Joe's steady bright gaze. "I've been in hospital. I'm not very fit yet have to rest for a time."

Joe stood aghast. Here stood a man he would have stood up in court and sworn to who said he wasn't Tom Penry when he was the spitting image of him and his sister Amy who lived in this very little village and whom he saw regularly. He decided to give the man the benefit of the doubt and play safe. He moved forwards again and held out his hand.

"Sorry about that. Pleased to meet anyways Jack. Glad somebody's using the cottage again; been empty long enough and tiz an old rule to anyone in need it be free. Can we help in any way?"

"No thanks. I'm alright on my own." He turned quickly to shut the door when Joe spoke again. As I recall there's no mattress for the bed. It's down at my cottage since Amy Treadle left." He looked hard at Jack as he spoke the name. "Tilly though it might get damp or the mice get in it. I'll bring it up ter night." If he thought the name might stir Jack he couldn't be more wrong. The man never moved a muscle.

"There's no need but thanks." He moved back inside and closed the door. The two men distinctly heard the key turn in the lock.

Joe scratched his grizzled head which was once bright red like his son's. He pulled his cap from his pocket and jammed it over his ears. They started back down the path.

"Well! I'll be a monkey's uncle if that isn't Tom Penry. What's up wi'ee? There's summate wrong ere, Mart. You mark my words."

Martin who had watched all and said nothing, now spoke. "I remember Tom well and I be sure there's summate wrong with 'im; a feeling yer know?"

"Yes lad, but don't be telling Ma till I gets a chance to speak. She's going to be hurt real bad if she thinks as her boy is back and he don't want to know us."

"What about Aunty Jan, Aunty Amy and the kids? We've got to do some serious thinking about what we tell 'em" Martin kicked a stone ahead of himself. They made their way home in silence. In the cottage Jack threw himself back in his chair, tears running silently down his cheeks into the hated beard.

Chapter 2

Rowan Berryman slid through the trees silent as a deer. She had practiced silent since she was very small, now had it to a fine art. She could get close to deer, squirrels and birds and often rescued injured ones, taking them to her small dispensary in the garden shed where she nursed them before releasing them back to the wild. Small and slender, with a thick mane of chestnut hair and large dark eyes set in an elfin face she was not unlike a fawn herself. She also had a determined chin with a dimple which showed she was not to be trifled with. Living in the forest as much as she did, she knew where the chaffinch had a nest, where the owl slept, who stole the best of the berries in the autumn, where the squirrel had his dray, where the biggest trout hid and where a mink lived. She knew the names of all the plants, flowers and trees around, where to find water when all the streams were dry and which field grew the best mushrooms. She knew much more than this but as she was as shy and quiet as any fawn, no one knew what or how much she did know.

As she fed birds in the winter, scattered hay for the deer which she bought from a neighbouring farmer, scattered food for the squirrels and kept a watch for predators, the birds allowed her to look in their nests, the squirrels skipped around her and deer stopped to stare before moving quietly away.

Rowen lived with her parents at the edge of the forest in a cottage called Wood cot. Her father Jed Berryman was gamekeeper for Arlington Hall while her mother Dora was seamstress for the ladies who lived there. She also made dresses for the village girls as well as her own family. Rowan had been their only child until Dora had discovered at forty five she was expecting, to her consternation but Jed's delight as he was hoping for a boy. Rowan was their delight and despair, delight as she was beautiful and took great care of them, working hard around the house, keeping herself by working a few days a week at the local vet's surgery and sketching illustrations for an author who wrote nature books. They despaired of her ever making friends or finding a boyfriend or getting a proper job as her father kept telling her to do. The rest of her time she roamed the woods collecting herb, flowers and sick animals.

She had always been a fey child, once when she was twelve she had been out rather late in the woods. There was a full moon which lit the clearing and a stag came out of the trees. She had caught her breath in wonder as for a few seconds she thought he was white and as he turned towards her she gasped; only Rowan could think that a single horn rose from his forehead. A cloud crossed the moon and he was gone. She might have told her mother but she had such a row for being out so late she didn't and never told anyone else either but she never forgot what she was sure she had seen.

Like many a shy person she was secretly interested in local goings on and today was no exception. She had already seen jack as she now knew him take his morning bath in the lake (a smile on her lips) followed him when he caught his trout (with admiration as this was one thing she could not do) and today she overheard the conversation between Joe Treggorran, who's family she knew well and viewed the new cottage tenant with puzzlement. She decided that life in the woods could be very interesting this spring.

She remembered the Penrys living at the cottage when she was in school, knew that Janet had opened a shop in St Austell and made pies and cakes until she married a vet and moved near Truro. Rowan and her mother had often called in for tea and cakes after shopping. It was still called 'Brambles' but was now run by Janet's one time partner Madseline who was married to a butcher Peter Knowles and they had a baby named Mark. Rowan also knew of Amy who had married Sep Treadle now living in Church Cottage since his mother died. They had five children and Amy cleaned the church. Sep was a charcoal burner. He also had jobs cutting and delivering firewood, sweeping chimneys and doing odd jobs in the village. Rowan used to see the charcoal burners but they had moved to the other side of the forest these last few years. Of course Rowan remembered Tom who she used to hero worship as a school girl. His bright curls, laughing blue eyes and good looks kept her peeping at him from behind trees whenever she could. Sometimes he would see her and call for her to come out. She never did.

Although she knew he had gone to war, this grey grizzled man could not be him. Tom could never look like that, he had never been shy he had always been whistling and singing about his work. Never mind, she would find out as she flitted about the woods. It would be fun, as long as this man didn't hurt the wildlife she would find out all about him. She hurried back towards home, time watching the men had made her late for her own jobs for she was due at the surgery for two o'clock where she would stay today until five. As she approached home she slid behind the trees which screened the shed from the yard, she had purposely designed it that way when it was being built so that she could be busy but no one in the yard could see her; very useful as now, Bill Wilkins horse was tied to the fence. Bill was a friend of her fathers, a man in his late thirties, six foot and big boned a dark brooding man with piecing black eyes, some Italian blood on his mother's side, her father thought. Rowan didn't like him and avoided him whenever possible. She felt her skin crawl and the hairs on the back of her neck rise like hackles whenever his black eyes rested upon her as they did whenever he was around her.

Her mother didn't like him either. She never said much as he was Jed's friend and had been for many years. He was a farmer, well off and was one of the guns when the Hall had a shoot. He had come more often since his wife died two years ago an Jed reckoned he was lonely. To be fair he had never said or done anything to upset Rowan and was always courteous to herself and her mother. He was considered to be a good man, a church deacon and always ready to help a friend.

"He has no family and we should accept him in friendship" This was in answer to Rowan's complain one Christmas when Bill had spent the day with them, barely taking his eyes off her all the time he was there. Dora had kept Rowan busy and close when he was around although she said little Rowan sensed Dora's dislike of him as well.

She tended her animals and made her way to the house to tidy herself for the surgery. To her relief Bill had gone. Calling to her mother that she was going she reached for her cycle in the porch when she heard her mother cry out, dropping the bike Rowan raced inside to find Dora doubled over an armchair in great pain.

"Mum! What's wrong? Is it the baby?"

"Ride for Nurse Beecham quickly. Tell her the baby is coming." Of course Rowan knew that her mother was expecting but she hadn't realised that it was imminent. She grabbed her bike and raced for the village wondering where her father was. Hot, flustered and shaking she knocked on Nan's door. Nan was the local midwife who had taken over when Mary Jordon had married and gone to live in Penzance. Nan Griffiths was an elderly single lady who had settled happily in Indian Queens. She joined the church, WI and the choir. A plump cheerful person she was soon in demand for all kinds of nursing jobs, tending the elderly and laying out as well as delivering babies.

"Oh! Hello Rowan. Mother on her way is she? I'll just get my bag and bike. You go on to work and try not to worry."

"Rowan told the vet the situation and hurried home again to find her father pacing the floor in agitation, pale and grim. Dora was on her bed labour well advanced. Rowan made tea for them all but Jed made no attempt to drink his.

"She's too old to e going through this. If anything goes wrong I'll never forgive myself."

Jed paced and muttered until Rowan could bare it no longer and fled the house to busy herself in her dispensary. Two hours later her father was shouting across the yard bringing her at a run.

"You've a brother Rowan. Ma's tired but come and see him"

Nan was tidying up. "All sorted, everything is fine he's a bonny boy. Mum's fine too. Everything went very smoothly considering your Mum's age and such a long time since you were born."

"Thank you Nan."

A red faced bundle lay in Dora's arms. Tiny hands reached out straight into Rowan's heart.

"Good for you Mum. He's beautiful. What are you going to call him?"

Jed sat beside the bed and reached for his son.

"I think Rowan should name him, don't you love?"

"I thought Ned but yes it's up to Rowan" Dora smiled with tired eyes.

Rowan looked at her parents with love and again at the eight pound boy who would take her place in childhood.

"I think Edward John Berryman is a very grand name. Then you can call him Ned"

Chapter 3

The thick mist which had hung around all morning was beginning to clear tops of bushes were becoming visible and Janet could see part of the garden. A neighbor had called to take James aged six and Dan who was four to a small school a couple of miles away. Dan being so young would be returned at lunch time.

Janet put the kettle on to make her husband Matt a cup of tea, he was a vet and being on call the night before deserved a lie-in. As she waited for the kettle to boil, she looked around with pleasure at her modern kitchen with its pretty curtains and gleaming copper pans. Gone were the days of the old black fireplaces where she did her cooking; first in the cottage in the woods and then in the back of her shop 'Brambles' in St Austell. Although Janet still had a few shares, Madseline had taken over when Janet married Matt. Baking had been Janet's mainstay in life after Amy, Tom and herself left their cruel lives in Devon fleeing to Cornwall where they came upon a ruined village with one small cottage intact where Jan was able to keep them with her sale of pies and cakes. They had lived on rabbit stews and veg from a small garden and had been content for a time.

Janet had suffered heartache after falling in love with a son of local gentry only to find that he was engaged to a wealthy young lady but wanted Janet as his mistress. She had sent him packing then concentrated on opening her shop with the help of Madeline a young local girl. They had remained firm friends ever since. Later Jan had met and married Matthew Jordon brother of the local midwife who had attended Amy when she got into trouble with a young charcoal burner and had to wed in a hurry. Matt and Janet went to work together at his father's veterinary practice where Janet was now receptionist rearing their two sons but her heart broke again when Tom went to war and she received the telegram missing presumed dead two years ago. Thinking of those days in the woods was the only real memories she had of him; her golden boy with laughing eyes and beautiful mouth. She know that he had to be dead, it was too long.

Amy had grieved too until her fifth child was born six months ago a blond blue-eyed child unlike her darker children. She had named him Thomas.

Janet made Matt's tea and took it to him. He roused and pulled her to him for a kiss. "I'll get up directly Darling mustn't waste my day off. Shall we go out somewhere?"

Janet was still down after thinking about Tom.

"Decide what you want to do while I get dressed. We'll pick Dan up from school on the way."

Janet went slowly downstairs and stood at the kitchen sink her mind still back at the ruined village. Suddenly she noticed two heads approaching up the drive. Heads only as the mist was still thick. One was a trilby hat and the other wide brimmed with a daisy on top. As they came into the clearing in front of the house she could see they were a man and a woman 'Poor Matt his day off gone" they probably wanted the vet. The man stepped forward and addressed her.

"Mrs Jordon?" he queried lifting his hat.

"Yes" Janet replied. For some reason her heartbeat quickened.

"Please excuse our calling without notice but we have some very important news for you. May we come in and speak privately?" Janet's heart began to race. "It's not the children is it?"

"No don't be alarmed. Quite a different matter entirely".

"You had better come in then." Janet closed the door and led them into t he parlour where a small fire burned sullenly in the tiled grate. Taking the man's hat she indicated chairs. The woman looked around before seating herself on one of the chintz covered armchairs while the man took a hard chair near the door. The woman Janet noticed was tall dressed in a brown coat her brown hair was coiled in loops under her hat with the daisy on it. She was very pale, her eyes large, grey, unsmiling. The man was rather shorter, grey haired and stout, looking rather anxious. He held out his card.

"I'm Hedley Tompkins, representing this lady who is Ruth Penry."

He held out his hand to Janet who took it without realising she did so her heart beating even faster her eyes fastened on the woman's face.

"I'm so sorry. Please sit down Mrs Jordon." The man's voice was solicitous and seemed to be coming from a distance.

"This is going to come as a shock I know but we had to come in person as soon as we found your address. We gathered your details from a shop in St Austell called 'Brambles' which I believe was yours at one time?"

"Never mind all that." Janet found her voice. "What has happened? Who is this woman?" Her eyes had never left the woman's face. She half opened her lips to answer but the solicitor was before her.

"If we are correct you are the elder sister of Thomas Penry are you not? Believed to have been reported missing in action in 1917. Am I right?"

"Yes, yes." She was finding it harder and harder to breathe. "Is there some news? Please. Please."

"Yes. Mr Penry or rather I should say Captain Penry is alive and well, that is to say we know he is alive but I fear that he is far from well."

Janet with a sob sat quickly down on the nearest chair. "I can't bear this. Where is he?"

The solicitor coughed, produced a large handkerchief and blew his nose loudly. Jan sat with her hands clenched tightly together. Ruth Penry never moved.

"I don't mean to worry you, Mrs Jordon but he left the hospital in Portsmouth without being discharged and disappeared. We have searched to no avail. We the found that he had a wife living in Truro who told us that he had sisters living in St Austell, we thought we might find him there."

"Wait! Wait!" Janet felt faint and feared that she was going to disgrace herself. She recovered with a great effort. "His wife?"

"The woman spoke for the first time."

"Yes Mrs Morgan. I'm sorry it comes as a shock but Tom and I were married four years ago before he was sent to France and you might as well hear it now but we have a little boy of two and a half"

Janet tried to speak and failed. Tears poured down her cheeks. Mr Thompkins rose "Can I call someone or get you some water?"

"Get Matt," Janet managed to get her tongue to work. "Please fetch my husband."

"No I'm here my love." Matt crossed to Jan's chair and knelt beside her. "I was coming downstairs and I heard."

"That Tom is alive."

"Good God, no I didn't hear that bit. Thank God but where is he?"

"This is the problem, Mr Jordon". Mr Tompkins shook hands with Matt. "As we said he has disappeared. We found Mrs Penry's address when he was brought to the hospital and she came at once but he refused to see her. A few days later he was gone."

Ruth Penry spoke in a low tone.

"I remembered he used to talk about you, Mrs Jordon. You kept the shop on St Austell and that your sister lived in Indian Queens but that is all I can remember. He said that we would visit you all when he came back so I'm afraid I didn't pay much attention though he did tell me he had been a charcoal burner in some forest where you were all living. He also talked about some people called Tregorrans. Might he have gone to them? Joe, Tilly and Old Len he called them. I'm sorry but t hat is all I have. We thought he may have come back to you or his other sister, we knew his memory had been affected that is the worry of it. I had no address so I went to see Mr Tompkins who is my father's solicitor. He found your shop and the lady there gave us your address and that of Mrs Treadle, we weren't able to get hold of her unfortunately and Mrs Knowles at the café advised us to come to you.

Janet had been turning paler all the while. Matt quickly fetched some water and spoke to their housemaid Gwen to fetch everyone tea.

"What do we do now?" Matt asked on his return.

"Well! We can only assume that he may have returned to his friends or his sister at Indian Queens and I suggest that we visit them and see what more we can find out and of course there is the cottage you were once living in, Mrs Jordon"

Jan had somewhat recovered. "Matt, we must pick up Dan and James wll be out at three thirty. We can't do much today it's too far."

Matt took hold of Jan's hand. He turned to Ruth. "Are you staying locally or do you have to return tonight?"

"No Peter is with my friend and staying the night as we didn't know what was happening so we booked in at a bed and breakfast nearby, friends of yours I believe a Mr and Mrs Farrell?" Matt stood up.

"Yes we know them well. You will be very comfortable there. Jan, I will see Mrs Penry and Mr Thompkins down to the farm and bring the boys back. If we could meet up in the morning as soon as the boys are in school, we could all drive up to the village and see what we can find out there. Does that fit with you all?"

They agreed and rose to leave. Ruth Penry held Janet's hand for a while. "I look forward to talking with you in more detail tomorrow if I may and you are not too upset?"

"I'm so thrilled that Tom is alive but dying of curiosity about your secret marriage and about your little boy?"

"We'll talk tomorrow and please call me Ruth."

Jan nodded, watched until they disappeared down the drive before heading to the kitchen where she sat on a hard dining chair and putting her hands to her face cried. Later when the boys had been fed, bathed and were in bed. Matt and Jan sat before the fire.

"I have great difficulty in keeping still Matt." Janet clasped and unclasped her hands agitatedly. "Do you think Tom would go back to the cottage? I know he can't be with

Amy or we would have hear by now or would he have gone to Joe and Tilly?"

"No dear, they would have got in touch before now with us or Amy. The cottage is the best bet but why wouldn't he come to us and if he's lost his memory he wouldn't remember about the cottage would he?"

Janet was becoming more and more agitated.

"Calm down Darling. We can't do anything before tomorrow and that will be here soon enough. There could be many reasons that we can't begin to think of. Don't forget he'll have been through a bad time and it's bound to have an effect on him."

"Oh! Matt! I'm so glad you couldn't go. Your chest and your flat feet saved you."

"I'm not glad when I think of all our lads out there. I feel such a failure."

"You are not a failure and your son went. He's out now, safe, engaged to be married and he has a good job so you should be proud, he did his bit for you and I'm glad he's safe home."

Janet loved Callum as her own and he had great love and respect for her. He called her Ma, got on well with his step family adored his step brothers and had a great time with them when he came to visit. They in turn regarded him as an uncle they were too young to remember Tom. Amy and Sep could not often visit so they didn't see much of their cousins. Will, Violet, Cissie, Richard and baby Thomas. They didn't often see Joe and Tilly Treggorran either although they all met up when they could. Joe's children were much older than Janet's and Amy's. Martin's now eighteen, Sammy seventeen, Issy almost sixteen and Emily twelve. They were mostly at work except Emily so they didn't see much of them. Matt's son Callum had been discharged from the

Navy six months ago and almost immediately found a job in a bank in Launceston, then a flat, two months ago he had fallen in love with a fellow cashier's daughter and was already engaged.

Although tired Janet couldn't sleep, at 2 o'clock Matt found her wandering the house. He packed her back to bed with a cup of hot milk to which he added more than a spoonful of brandy; she finally fell asleep.

Mr Tompkins and Ruth Penry arrived the next morning at nine on the dot. James and Dan were dispatched to school with a neighbour who would collect Dan at midday and James at three when she collected her own, they then set off for Indian Queens. Janet had tried phoning her sister via the village shop but the girl came back saying there was no one at Church cottage although she had seen Sep taking the two older children to school before he went to work but couldn't hear anyone in the house. With that Jan had to be content until she could be there herself. Mr Thompkins was a very steady driver but rather slow and it was almost lunch time before they pulled up at Amy's cottage which showed no signs of life. Knowing Amy cleaned the church. Janet suggested they tried there although how she managed with two little ones and a baby she didn't know. As she pushed at the heavy doors, she was met with the smell of polish and fresh flowers. The brass shone, the candles stood ready for lighting on the altar but of Amy there was no sign.

When they called at the vicarage they were told by the housekeeper that the vicar had been called away on urgent business and she hadn't seen Amy since yesterday afternoon when she had cleaned the church but come to think of it she hadn't been around the village for a couple of days before that. Her husband had been seen taking the older ones to school these last two or three mornings and picking them up at night.

"We had better have some lunch at the Inn" Matt pulled his coat together as it started to rain. "We are going to have a to wait for Sep to come home, he'll pick the kids up at half three, we might as well wait in comfort."

"Couldn't we go to Joe's or up to Blackberry Cottage?" Janet begged.

"We are hungry and it's starting to rain; better to eat first and wait for Sep he'll know if anybody's been about the woods or we could call on Tilly later, may save us that long walk for nothing."

Reluctantly Jan agreed and they headed for the inn half hoping to meet Amy or Tilly on the way. The inn was full of strangers to Janet but she looked around with interest. It was under different management since Janet had first sold her blackberry pies here, it seemed a long time ago. The new people had redecorated and it was very clean and attractive. Her heart jolted a little when she remembered it was here she had first met Geoffrey Arlington the young aristocrat who had been her first love and broken her heart. It seemed so long ago now. They ordered and found the food excellent.

"We could do with one of your pies on the menu now." Matt teased her for he had been told of the blackberry pie that had given the Penry's their first income. Refreshed they returned to Church cottage. Still no one at home and the door was locked. They were standing undecided whether to go to Tilly's house or whether to chance a walk through the forest to Blackberry Cottage as the Penry's had always called it, when Janet saw Sep approaching with William and Violet. Upon them spotting Jan they raced to throw themselves at her almost knocking her down in their enthusiasm. "Steady on," Janet hugged them to her.

As she had been at the birth of both Will and Violet, they held a special place in her heart. Amy had been alone in her troubles and Janet had left her business to care for her until Sep and Amy had taken over their responsibilities along with the tenancy of the cottage when Jan had been able to return to her own life and her shop.

Will was now a sturdy eight year old and a replica of his father while Violet at six and a half was petite, blond with the most amazing pair of violet eyes hence her name, "Where's your Mam?" Janet asked holding them from her.

"Gone off" answered Will now attaching himself to Matt.

"Gone off? What do you mean gone off?" Jan turned to Sep who looked haggard and pale.

"She upped and left two days ago," He answered. "She does every now and then".

"Why? Whatever are you saying? Has she left you altogether?" Janet had never heard of this. "Do you mean she has done this before?"

"Once or twice." Sep was evasive, glancing wonderingly at the two strangers. "You had better come in although I am ashamed at the state of the house." As it was raining again it seemed a good idea but as they entered the cottage Janet wasn't so sure. She quickly introduced the solicitor and Ruth while Mr Thompkins tried to explain everything to Sep who appeared to be only half listening, Janet looked around. The state of the house was appalling. The fire hadn't been lit for a while yet the grate was full of ashes and half burnt sticks, the table loaded with breakfast things, bottles and jars. The sink full of dirty dishes and saucepans presumably from last night's dinner. Clothes littered every chair and cupboard while wet baby things hung from a rack and the floor was filthy. The open parlour door showed that room to be in the same state littered with clothes and toys. Janet heard a soft gasp from Ruth and a discrete cough from the solicitor. She turned on Sep.

"What is going on? It was never like this. Where is she? What's been happening here?" Sep knelt to clear the grate and light the fire keeping his back to them.

"We had a row. Amy is not good in the house and I couldn't stand anymore and told her so. She complained that she never had fun anymore or a moment to herself and that she was going,"

"Where can she go Sep?" Janet was on point of collapse, first Tom and now this. "She goes up to Pelham. There are some new houses there and she's made friends with a Molly Dunne; she's got kids too. I don't know what her husband does but he seems to be a way a lot though I think he may be in the Merchant Navy, anyways she and Amy as thick as thieves and that's where she will have gone."

"There's something else that you're not telling us isn't there? I can see by your face." Sep had lit the fire and got up to put the kettle on. He looked as if he hadn't slept and was very pale.

"You had better hear it all," he said grimly. He cleared chairs for them to sit down. Will and Violet went to play in the parlour. "That Molly's got a brother. They call him Bran short for Branwell or some such fancy name. Well! He's always there and in Amy's eyes he can do no wrong. It's always Bran this and Bran that. I'm sick of it so I told her she had better go and live with them and let him keep her. I'm tired Janet. I've not had any sleep since she went two days ago, apparently she came back to do the church, she always does that right enough, money in it see. She complains I don't give her enough. I can't work any harder. I do the charcoal burning and it's further to go now it's the other side of forest. I cut logs and sell them, sweeps chimneys, digs old folks gardens and our own. She doesn't have to anything only look after us lot and do church,"

"What happened to the girl I paid to help her."

"Oh! She got rid of her said she were making eyes at me and pinching stuff. I never see that."

"You say it has happened before?" interrupted Matt

"Once or twice a couple of years back, she promised it wouldn't happen again and I believed her." Before the horrified Janet could say anything Matt spoke.

"Look I have to be in surgery tomorrow and I'm sure Mrs Penry and Mr Thompkins have obligations tomorrow as well. I suggest that Jan stops here, I go home sort the boys out and come back for you in a day or two. It will give Janet time to find Amy and any news of Tom around the village. Would that suit you Mrs Penry?"

"Fine by me, I'll go back and see to Peter, I can't leave him any longer. If Mr Thompkins will be so kind as to see me home I would be grateful."

"Of course I will my dear and I should get back to the office."

Ruth turned to Janet. "I'm so sorry to leave you with this dreadful situation, but could I come and see you when you return home, then we can talk some more? I know you will be in touch should you find anything out."

Janet took her hand and kissed her. "Of course I will and you will be most welcome." Matt kissed his wife, shook hands with Sep, telling Jan he would be back in a couple of days and they left. Janet was left dazed by recent events so after helping Sep clean up and feed the children she took herself to the spare room closing the door with a sigh of thankfulness.

Chapter 4

Janet woke to the sound of heavy rain beating the window. There was no way she was going to find Amy until it eased. What was wrong with everybody? She should be happy that Tom was alive even if he wasn't well; now Amy had to disappear leaving a right mess behind her.

It was too wet to go to the Treggorrans or to Blackberry cottage to see if Tom was there. She had heard Sep leave with the children so she had the place to herself. She went downstairs to make tea and toast. Fair play to Sep he had lit the fire and cleared the table. Janet gathered all the dirty clothes she could find and put the boiler on. When the water heated she cleared everything away and washed the many pots and dishes, scrubbed the table and washed the floor. Looking in the pantry she saw plenty of shopping needed doing as well. That would have to wait. Two hours later the washing was done and through the mangle, spread on a clothes horse in the scullery, on the rack above the fire and on a line she found in the outhouse.

The rain stopped at lunchtime so Janet borrowed one of Sep's macs and Amy's wellies. The village shop provided most of her needs, the butcher next door a scraggy end of mutton, sausages, bacon and two dozen eggs. Sep kept a good garden so potatoes, onions and carrots were in store in his shed. Back at the cottage she made enough stew to last a couple of days, a large fruit cake and two apple pies. She found a rabbit Sep had hung in the shed. She skinned it, stuffed it with onions wrapped it in fat bacon and put it in the oven, boiled some potatoes and leaving a note for Sep, dressing again in mac and wellies set off in search of her sister.

It was a fair walk to Pelham and Janet was feeling tired when she reached the small hamlet. Looking around she saw the six new houses that had been built on a meadow well away from the old farm cottages which huddled around a small chapel. As Sep had told her Molly's house was the third one along she went to the door and knocked. The sound of children playing came to her and she knocked again. The door was opened by a plump young woman of about thirty years. Her tousled black hair framed a face which was quite pretty but spoiled by the sulky motion. She wore men's slippers and filthy apron. "Hello is Amy here?" asked Jan peering past her.

"Who wants to know?" The woman asked almost aggressively.

"I believe you maybe Molly and my sister is staying with you."

"Amy!" screeched the woman. "Someone here wants yer."

"If its Sep, Tell him –" Amy came rushing through the house stopping short as she spotted Janet. "Oh! It's you Jan"

"Yes it's me and I need to speak to you urgently."

Can she come in?" Amy asked Molly who showed no signs of moving out of the door way.

"No need if Molly would be so kind as to look to your babies for a few minutes we can speak out here." Molly turned back inside and shut the door.

"What's the matter?" Amy's face was white. "If Sep's got you up here to chase after me he's wasting his time."

Janet caught hold of her arm. "Now you look here Madam. I know you have a lot to do with five youngsters at your heels but you aren't a young girl any more playing at house. Why are you here instead of seeing to your home and family?"

"I am too tired and Sep keeps nagging that I don't keep the house right and the kids are too noisy, He doesn't help, he's either out all the time or shouting at me."

"So! You intend to stay here with this woman and her kids and don't tell me she does much housekeeping, I'll bet she's got you doing half of it, rather be here would you instead of that lovely little cottage, a job you enjoy doing, lovely children healthy and beautiful and a man that loves you and works all the hours God sends to keep you all in food? You don't know that you are born."

"I just like to come and have a drink and a laugh with Molly; some time to my self"

"What about that brother of hers Bran, I believe his name is?"

"He's Molly's brother, he plays with the kids and makes me laugh. He's been over the world and is interesting to talk to. That's all we do, talk, have a laugh and a drink."

"You always were a selfish little madam. Not much change there then. Now you listen to me and listen well. Sep is a good, good man. He works his heart out to provide for you all. He doesn't get time to chat with friends, go for a drink or enjoy his family and you pay him off by running away to enjoy yourself leaving him with even more work and worry. Your house is filthy and the little ones need their mother and father and miss their brother and sister. You have a lovely home if you would only clean it. Mrs Treadle left you all her lovely things and you treat it all like rubbish. You clean the church, it's beautiful, and your house should be the same. All Sep's ma's brass and china were left to you. How many girls get that chance? She would turn in her grave if she could see it now. You are an ungrateful wretch. Sep needs food ready for him, clean dry clothes, someone to be interested in what he does and some love. If you don't love him you should at least respect him for what he does for you all. What happened to the girl I paid to help you out?"

Amy burst into noisy sobs. "I sent her away, she was making eyes at Sep and she took things. I can't cope Jan, Tommy is only six months old, it's all too much."

"You listen to me. You grow up and take responsibility. Take charge of things. You should have tackled her about it. Sep hadn't noticed her at all but he will notice someone if you don't pull yourself together. He's a good looking man, he would soon find someone to look after him and be a companion to him. She might tempt him to leave the children with you and go off with her. How would you cope them? You could lose everything. Is that what you want? I don't believe he would do such a thing but you never know when a man's fed up he might start looking around him."

"No but I don't know what to do." Amy walled.

"Well! It's certainly not staying here with this woman who looks as if she wants someone to take on her problems. Is that going to be you?" the door opened. "Are you going to feed these babies or not?" Molly shouted.

"Times getting on and I have to fetch Harry from school. I can't leave Sue here."

"What do you usually do." asked Janet. Molly looked her up and down insolently.

"Put her in the pushchair and take her, why?"

"Well you will just have to do that today. My sister and I are going home."

Janet marched into Molly's house which was in much the same state as Amy's. There was no sign of Bran thankfully. Cissie and Ricky as they called Richard; ran to hug Jan clinging around her knees. Cissie began to cry "I want to see Dadda." At three she was a pretty dark haired child with her father's eyes. Ricky was brown haired, brown eyes and very quiet rather as Tom had been. Baby Thomas was asleep in his pram, his blond downy head just showing over the grubby blanket. Molly's little girl Sue ran to her mother who picked her up. "Don't come up here anymore Amy I don't want the bother of people looking for yer. Best we meet down the village."

Amy's pride came to the fore as she packed her stuff in the pram. "Don't bother; it's all too much. I can manage without any of you. Thanks for having us. See you around." She swung Ricky on to the seat of the pram while Janet carrying Cissie they set off down the road. They walked in silence for a while, Janet still seething and Amy sulking.

"Have these children been fed? I can see Tommy has but what about these two and they smell as if they want a good bath,"

"Don't keep going on Jan. Of course they've been fed they had bread jam and cake at lunchtime."

"I'll keep on until you pull yourself together and there'll be no more Bran this and that in front of Sep he doesn't deserve it." They walked in silence until the church came in sight. Ahead they could see Sep slowly walking home with Will and Violet. Their steps were slow and Violet dragged her satchel in the road. Sam his head down looked defeated.

"Take a good look lady. I had some good news for you but I don't think you deserve to know."

"What news?" Amy straightened up and began to walk more quickly while Cissie ran to catch up with her siblings. Ricky had fallen asleep in his seat.

"Never mind now just get in the house and get these all fed. There's roast rabbit in the oven and the veg only needs heating."

Sep's face lit up when he saw them going to Amy he took her in his arms.

"I'm sorry Sweetheart. I didn't mean to be nasty to you but I get tired and fed up as well. Are you back to stay? I've missed you and the little ones."

"You're too soft Sep." Janet marched in and began lifting the roast out of the oven and pushing the potatoes over the fire. "I'd throw her out without the children get someone else to look after you all. She's always been the same; selfish."

Amy threw herself at Sep. "I'm not really I'm not and I'm sorry. I can see Jan's been busy. The house looks nice and I can do it. I can."

"Of course you can it's only since Tommy's been born, you've got run down. I'll get better I'll help," Janet turned around from where she was dishing up.

"Look you two. I'm sorry too. It's a lot of work I know. I'll pay for help again for you but I will pick her and there'll be no more of this nonsense." Sep put his arms around her, "Thank you Jan for all your help I do appreciate it. I really am very grateful."

"Me too and I'm sorry." Amy hugged them both.

"Right call the children, we'll eat, then I have some news for both of you. We have another mission and I'll need both your help this time."

Chapter 5

It seemed as if winter was well and truly over. Blue skies appeared every morning with fluffy white clouds and a gentle breeze. The temperature grew warmer and warmer. The woods were full of windflowers, violets and primroses and deep under the trees bluebells formed a blue lake. Birds nested and squirrels routed for last year's nuts among the leaves. The trees were putting on their green gowns while butterflies and bees worked their way from flower in search of honey and nectar.

Rowan had been looking after mother and baby brother for the last week or so but now Dora's sister Jean had come from Wiltshire and was to stay until Dora was fit again. Baby Ned was strong and thrived, feeding and sleeping. His father doted on him and had been seen pushing the baby in his pram as far as the woodland gate.

"He wouldn't do that when you were a baby" laughed Dora. "He adored you but was very sensitive about it." Rowan was glad. It meant she was now free to wander the woods again. She met Martin Treggorran and they discussed as to whether Jack was really Tom. Martin was sure but Rowan needed more sightings to be really certain. She slipped among the trees to the cottage. There was no smoke from the chimney this morning and all was quiet so Rowan risked a peep over the garden wall, to her surprise the garden had been cleared and dug. A bonfire was doing a great job of burning couch grass. A patch had already been planted. She could see lined rows with sticks at each end with seed packets stuck on them. Washing hung on the line, Jack or whoever he was had made himself at home. She waited a while then moved through the woodland paths listening for anyone about. She wandered down to the lake and wasn't surprised to see Jack swimming strongly through the murky waters. Rowan sometimes had a wicked streak and for a moment thought of two outrageous ideas; the first to take his clothes which were neatly folded on the bank and hide them. The second was to join him in the water and shock him. She dismissed both and hoped that he hadn't seen her. Moving softly she hid carefully behind a large beech tree and waited.

Jack had seen her or rather a glimpse of somebody and stayed in the water as long as possible. When there was no movement on the bank he came out, hurried dried himself, dressed and picked up the trout he had earlier caught and started back to the cottage. As Rowan moved around the tree with misjudgement they came face to face.

"Hello." Rowan smiled shyly. "Sorry to have disturbed you."

For some reason Jack faced Rowan without that dreadful feeling coming from over him. It felt more like seeing a deer or a fox. Her shy attitude and fawn like movements calmed rather than frightened him. When he looked in her face he saw only a calm beauty.

"Hello." He said. "You're not disturbing me but I must go home now."

"Good bye." Rowan slipped away through the trees leaving Jack puzzled but not alarmed. She looked vaguely familiar but he didn't want to call her back to find out. Back at the cottage he cooked his fish but couldn't eat so he pulled a bag from under a table taking out a pair of sharp scissors and a shaving set. Earlier he had made his way into St Austell with eyes down, kept well away from 'Brambles' and shopped in the far part of the town picking up supplies he needed and several garments for he was short of clothes; as he shopped he kept his head down and avoided speaking more than was necessary. He had found a Post Office and been able to draw some money. Thankfully his pass book had been in his greatcoat pocket with a few other papers. He was thankful that he had been able to bring it from the hospital where he had found it at the end of his bed. After this expedition he had returned to the cottage soaked with sweat and unable to stop shaking. He dropped off his shopping and headed for the lake where after catching a fish for supper he swam for a while to calm himself down. Back at the cottage an hour later, clean-shaven with his hair cut, he sat still trembling in his chair. He felt clean and very different; looking at himself in a mirror he had found in one the chests the tears ran down his cheeks. "It's me, I'm back." He murmured and fell asleep without dreaming.

It was dark when he awoke and the owl was back in the tree with a tentative 'Twit and a long woo' but no strange noises came from the cottage only the smell of fish as Jack reheated his dinner and cut slices of bread and jam. Later he sat wondering about the girl he had seen and wondered why she hadn't bothered him as everyone else did. He had noticed that she was brown haired, brown eyed and pretty. He voice had been soft and low and she hadn't wanted to stay and talk; strangely he was grateful to her for that. He just couldn't face seeing his sisters or their families. Too dangerous; he was only just emerging from a very dark place, better to face it alone or he might never come out. He settled himself to sleep but later the owl was again sent packing by shouts and cries deep in the night.

Rowan made her way home keeping an eye out for animals or birds that might need her attentions. She didn't have many patients at the moment so there wasn't much to do in her dispensary. Picking up a baby bird that had fallen from the nest she returned it to its agitated parents and demanding siblings. She laughed at their open breaks, depositing an insect she found into an open mouth. "I hope that helps." She said, speaking aloud to the finch parent that chattered at her angrily above her head. She had few patients to care for, a blackbird who had a broken wing but was now almost ready to fly again, a mouse with a hurt foot and a pair of baby pigeons who had lost their parents. After feeding them and closing up for the night she crossed the yard and came face to face with Bill Wilkins who was tying his horse to the fence.

"Hello! My pretty maid" He spoke in a soft ingratiating tone which Rowan hated "Where have you been? Leaves in your hair?" He put up a hand to remove them. She flinched and backed away. "I think you have been up to no good in these woods. We'll have to keep an eye on you." He placed an arm around her resisting shoulders as they entered the house. Her father was about to open the door and Bill dropped his arm.

"Good evening Jed, how's that new boy coming along?" The two men entered the kitchen while Rowan fled to her room just putting her head around her mother's door where she and Aunt Jean were feeding and changing little Ned.

"That Bill's here." Rowan pulled a face. "I'll have my tea when he's gone. "Her aunt looked up from nappy folding. "Who is he?" she asked.

"He's nobody really. See you later." Rowan was gone. Jean looked inquiringly at her sister. Dora frowned. "He's a friend of Jed's. Rowan and I don't care for him but in Jed's eyes he can do no wrong. He's a warm man very well off, gentleman farmer I suppose you'd call him. He's only thirty five although he looks older. His wife died two years ago and Jed thinks that he would be good for Rowan but I don't; she's too young, shy and gentle for the likes of him. I only wish Jed wouldn't go encouraging him."

Her sister smiled. "I think Rowan can take care of herself, she always seems to slip away from things that she doesn't like."

"I know but that Bill is persistent. I wish she could meet someone else. Martin Treggorran would be better although he is a bit young but better than Bill." They turned back to Ned who was now demanding his dinner.

Bill settled himself in the deep armchair as Jed handed him a glass of beer. "That little maid of yours does like to take herself off into the woods doesn't she? Aren't you worried now she is old enough to wed that someone out there might spoil her chances?"

"Rowan knows those woods backwards. I'd like to see the man that could find her if she didn't have a mind."

Bill drank his beer slowly. "Better you get her married off; a child or two would settle her down. I've never said a word to you or her about it but I have a mind to take her on myself – with your permission Jed of course and if she's willing. We would want a month or two to get to know each other of course."

Jed stared at him. "I didn't know that you felt like that Bill?"

"No offence Jed but I've always thought her a pretty young thing and been going to say something. Surely she's a bit old to be messing about with animals, birds and such nonsense. They usually get over that sort of thing when they are about nine or ten me and my sister did."

Jed hesitated sipping his beer. "I'll be honest Bill I did think that she might have grown out of all this forest stuff and find a lad by now but it don't seem to happen. Maybe if she's willing to talk with you could; as you say get to know each other better. See how it goes, mind to be honest I think you be a bit old for her but maybe that's what she needs."

Bill rose pleased with his visit. "I'll take my time and not scare her seeing as how you agree. She'll not want for anything mind, I've plenty."

They shook hands and as they left the house Bill turned to Jed. "You know there' a fellow over in Penry's cottage don't you? Don't know who he is yet; calls himself Jack Travers, wouldn't trust him. I don't think that Rowan should go too far until we sees what he's about. What do you think?"

"I'll warn her. Some say its Tom Penry back but that's unlikely or his sisters would be over here or he'd stay with them. Thanks Bill I'll tell her." They shook hands again and Bill mounted up and left. Rowan heard him go and with a sigh of relief came down to help with dinner and play with her new brother.

Chapter 6

Amy could barely contain her excitement on hearing that Tom was alive and was all for going to the Treggorran's to find out what they knew also to the cottage to see the man living there. As soon as Will and Violet were in school she had the younger ones fed, dressed and they were ready to go. They found Joe and Tilly at home as Joe was making repairs to the hen house after a fox had pushed his way in and killed all but three. Sammy and Martin had left for the charcoal burning and Emily was at school.

"Is he here? Is he here? Is it true?" gasped Amy flinging her arms around Tilly who grew plumper and merrier as she grew older.

"Oh! Tiz lovely to see you both again" Tilly hugged her back and kissed Janet. "Who are you looking for?"

"Hello there." Joe came over swinging a hammer. "That should stop Mr Fox. How are you girls? Lovely ter see yer and the little ones, don't they grow fast Till?"

"Yes they do. Come away in and have a cake and a cup of tea, won't be as good as yours though Jan."

"We will in a while. Joe do you think the man you have in the cottage might be Tom but it wouldn't be like him not to come to you or us? I can hardly dare hope it's too much to take in."

"Let's go to the cottage now. We would know if it's Tom at once, no matter how he looks now." Amy was already out of the gate.

"We'll come with you, won't you Joe? We'll give a hand with the little ones. There's our old pushchair 'twill save Ricky's legs. He and Cissie can take turns."

The party set off bringing many memories back for Janet and Amy of this track through the woods and of blackberry picking in the autumn. They slowed down as they came near the cottage and hesitated on seeing the smoke from the chimney. It felt very strange approaching what had once been their home. They walked up the path and Joe knocked sharply on the door. There was no reply.

"Perhaps he's out." Amy whispered. Joe knocked again then tried the door, it was locked. "No one here, we should have brought a note."

"There is, I just saw a face behind the curtain" shrieked Amy, "Tom it's us. Please, please open the door." There was no reply.

"What can we do?" asked Tilly "if he won't show 'isself we've had it"

Janet walked to the window and rapped sharply. "Excuse me but we are looking for Tom Penry. Please just tell us if you are him or know of him. He's our brother and we have only just heard that he is alive. We have missed him so much. We just want to know if he has been seen around here because it is where he used to live, we won't bother you; just tell us who you are." There was no sound from the cottage.

If they could have seen the man huddled on the floor, they would have been shocked. Curled in a heap sobbing, he shook; willing himself to get up to open the door and falling. 'There are too many people, too many people.' He murmured through his tears. 'Forgive me, I just can't; not now.'

Janet turned away tears streaming down her face. "I did so hope." She sobbed on Tilly's shoulder. Amy sobbed out loud. "I'm not giving up. I'll find you." She shouted into the woods. Joe led them home cursing to himself that the man hadn't had the courage enough to answer a few questions. He just knew it was Tom and something was very wrong indeed that he couldn't admit to it.

They returned to Amy's house where Janet helped her sort out cupboards and drawers before walking to the butchers buying bones and a scrag of mutton. She had a chat with Mrs Grace the butcher's wife who was a great gossip knowing all that went on in the village. On her advice she crossed the road to a row of thatched cottages overlooking the green. When she knocked on the door of number four it was opened by a middle aged woman with a smiling face. She wore a floral apron over a green dress, her graying hair in a tight bun.

"Good afternoon Mrs Taylor. I'm Janet Jordon." The woman laughed, hazel eyes alight. "Of course I remember you; Janet Penry who married the vet. How are you this long time? Do come in."

Janet stepped into a pleasant room smelling of polish, brasses gleamed and windows shone, she crossed he fingers that this woman would help Amy. They had a cup of tea while Janet explained about Tom's disappearance and Amy's problems.

"You must be worried sick about it all. Of course I can help. I am looking for a couple of days a week as Mrs Grace probably told you and I remember Amy marrying Sep, always a polite well-mannered boy. Little Violet always waves to me on her way to school. I will certainly go and see her, we'll arrange something."

"Thank you so much I will pay you each month myself if you don't mind sending me detail of your hours. I'm afraid Amy isn't good with money. Here is my address, we are on the telephone if you could give me a ring and I will send it straight away, shall we say the end of each month?"

"That will be fine and I hope to see you at Amy's sometimes." They chattered a little more before Janet left in time to see Matt's car pull up at the cottage. Amy threw her arms around her sister with tears in her eyes.

"Thank you Jan for all your help, yes I know Mrs Taylor; she used to work in the shop years ago. I think I could get on well with her."

"Well, don't take advantage, she was good enough to offer to babysit now and then so that you and Sep can go out together and keep away from that Molly and her brother as much as possible. You will if you have any sense that is."

Janet turned to Sep. "I know you will keep an eye out for Tom; tell me anything you can find out. I wish I could stay longer but the boys need me. The Treggorrans are watching out too. I am so worried that he may be ill."

Sep hugged her and kissed her cheek. "Don't worry, Joe and I will do what we can. Thank you for all you have done for Amy. We do appreciate it." He shook hands with Matt who turning his pockets out found several packets of sweets and a bag of modelling clay to the delight of the children.

"Well!" Matt said as they drove off. "You have sorted Amy out but what about Tom? We aren't much nearer solving that mystery. Ruth Penry came by. I gave her lunch but she couldn't stay any later because of the boy but she is coming again soon to talk to you. I asked her to bring Peter and to stay a day or two, if that's alright with you?"

"Of course it is." Janet replied. "I can't wait to meet him, Tom's son. I wonder if he knows about him."

She settled in her seat with mixed emotions. Still worried about her brother, so glad that he was at least alive; hoping that Amy would stop her silly ways and settle down, most of all relief at going home to her darling boys with Matt at her side.

Chapter 7

Rowan moved silently through the trees, her heart heavy her eyes full of tears. She failed to understand why her father should suddenly have the idea that Bill Wilkins would make her a suitable husband. She didn't want suitable and she didn't want a husband either and certainly not Bill Wilkins. She had never liked him and lately she had felt threatened by him, maybe it was the way he kept staring at her even with her parents in the room, she was even more sure that he stalked the woods looking for her several times; she had thought she heard him but her own woodcraft was better than his and she had slipped away without stopping to find out.

She often watched Jack catch his fish or have a swim, without him seeing her but one day she came upon him suddenly as he sat on a log in a clearing. It was too late to take evasive action as she came out of a copse just in front of him.

"Hello." She said. "I'm sorry to disturb you."

"That's alright," replied Jack. His first instinct was to get up and run but the small slip of a girl with the eyes of a fawn seemed to pose no threat. He stayed where he was.

"You are Jack aren't you? My name's Rowan, you know like the tree." She smiled a shy sweet smile that lit her small face like a ray of sunlight. "I'll go and leave you in peace.

Jack cleared his throat which felt rusty with disuse. "That's alright." He said again. "It's usually me that goes when anyone comes. I sometimes see you in the woods. You keep out of sight don't you? Like me."

Rowan sat down rather nervously on a tree stump nearby. "Yes I like to see the wild things and you can't if you don't hide."

"I know. It's good to see them." Jack felt safe with this fey child of the woods no images spoilt the beauty of her face or voice. His soul remained calm.

"I've been sitting here watching two squirrels, they have forgotten where they left their stores." Jack mused.

"They are always doing that." Rowan replied. "I sometimes bring nuts and berries and scatter them for them to find."

"Do you now? You often walk these woods then?" Rowan found herself telling him about her dispensary and the animals that she looked after. Jack was content to listen to her soft voice talking about the things that he loved for the first time finding solace in someone's company. They talked awhile until sticks crackling in the undergrowth brought both to their feet. Rowan slipped away through the trees while Jack turned for home. Feeling a little disappointed that their talk had been interrupted but then it wouldn't do to become too friendly and there were other people about he could sense it and it wasn't safe. He returned to his cottage and locked the door.

It was two weeks later that Rowan found the dog. He was running through the village, dirty, hungry, and thin. The village shop was annoyed that he had overturned their dustbins. Mrs Dunrose who lived at number eight had been feeding him until everyone carried on at her that she was encouraging him and he would always be a nuisance. When Rowan went to deliver her illustrations to Ralph Conway's home, she found him trying to coax the dog with a bone. As she approached the dog made a sudden grab for it and ran off.

"I feel sorry for him but I can't get near he's too frightened. You should have a go you're good at this sort of thing." He smiled as he took Rowan's folder.

"Does no one look for him?" she asked as she pocketed the little envelope he always had ready for her.

"No he's been running around for the last three weeks or more. That gives me an idea. Would you like to sketch me some dogs and some wolves? I'm doing a book on the differences between dogs, wolves, foxes, etc. I'll take some of those too if you don't mind. About six dogs I think and a couple of wolves and two of foxes". Rowan laughed. "I'll do my best, any particular breed?"

"No I'll leave it to you." His eyes twinkled. "Mix them up." He called after her.

Rowan smiled to herself. He was always doing some new project and it made him very interesting to work for. The dog was chewing his bone under a bench on the green as she walked by. She stopped to look at him.

"Hello boy you look in a bad way. You need some good food, a bath and some treatment by the look of you. That's a nasty cut on your face, has someone thrown something at you? Why don't you come home with me?" She held out a hand but the dog growled and worried at his bone. She went to the butcher begging some scraps in a bowl and held it out to him talking all the while in a soft tone. The dog smelled meat and advanced a little way towards her. Coaxing in a soft voice she gradually got a little closer and with great patience she managed to get him to eat out of the bowl in her hand. Two days later he was in her dispensary tucking into two good meals a day and sleeping in a warm box. She took advice from the surgery giving him a course of antibiotics with his food. She found he was good natured and had a lovely black and tan coat with four white feet when she finally got him in a bath. Wormed and de-loused he came to life and she realised he was quite a young dog not more than two at the most. He objected at first to a collar and lead until he realised they led to long walks in the woods. Rowan named him Skip because that is what he did while she prepared his meals or took down his lead. Her parents didn't want him in the house so she built him a pen onto the shed where he could wander in and out but fenced away from her patients. One thing thrilled her, he didn't like Bill and Bill didn't like him either and told her to get rid of him.

"He's probably got disease, a mongrel like that and he'll bite somebody one day and have to be put down, so get rid before you get too fond."

"I'll not." argued Rowan hotly. "He's not yours, he's mine so mind your own business and leave me alone."

Bill's lips tightened and he scowled at her. "If I see him around my land and loose through the woods I'll shoot him so keep him shut up or find someone to have him. You'll not be bringing him to my house."

"I'm not coming to your house so there." Rowan tossed her head and led Skip away vowing that she would keep him on a lead forever rather than risk him being shot. How she hated the man. She wished he would stay from her but with her father's encouragement he seemed to be here more than ever.

It was a month later at Ned's christening her worst fears were brought to light. She found Ned's godparents were to be Dora's best friend Celia Barnet and her husband Ronald with Bill Wilkins as the second godfather. Her heart sank he would have every excuse to be around more than ever.

Her mother dressed in a new green dress and hat was so pleased to be holding her new longed for son and showing him off to friends and neighbours. Rowan couldn't bring herself to say a word although she did confide her fears to her aunt Jean who gave her a hug and told her not to worry, things would sort themselves out. Rowan may have been reassured until she heard her father's speech at the meal afterwards.

"Silence everyone please. Thank you all for coming and for your gifts. We never thought to see this day but thank the Lord we have. We don't often have chance to get together like this but it's time we did. There might be another do before long when our lovely daughter Rowan gets wed as we think she will (if our Bill here has anything to do with it)." Everyone laughed. "it won't be long hopefully so raise your glasses to the future and to Master Edward John Berryman or Ned as we call him." Everyone toasted, cheered and applauded while Rowan stood rooted to the spot, the blood frozen in her veins, her eyes wide with horror as people began to congratulate her. As soon as her legs would carry her she fled from the hall.

Chapter 8

The next few days Rowan kept out of sight as much as possible. Dora had been furious with Jed after the speech. When she tackled him that night, he laughed.

"I don't know what you are so het up about. It would be good for the lass to get rid of some of her fey ways and messing about. She wouldn't have to get a job. Bill's a warm man a couple of children would settle her. She wouldn't want for anything."

"She doesn't love him and I don't trust him. I think she would land herself in a very hard loveless marriage. She also dislikes him intensely." Dora was almost in tears. "Look how you embarrassed her in the village."

"Jed slowly lit his pipe. "She'll get over it. She can't run wild in the woods for ever and that animal thing is only a hobby like those drawing things for that artist fellow. Anyway if she hates him that much she'll turn him down."

"Oh! Jed can't you see what's in front of your eyes? Bill will nag and keep on at her until she doesn't know what's what. I don't trust him. His wife was a timid cowering sort of woman and I always wondered why."

"Oh! Get away with you woman. Go and see to our son. Rowan's old enough to look after herself." He turned away picking up his paper. Rowan meantime tended her animals and worried. For the next week or two she spent as much time at the vet's surgery as she could and sketched the dog sketches for Ralph. She took Skip with her when she delivered them. Ralph was pleased to see him looking so well and beautifully groomed.

"That's all he needed love and attention. Good girl, these sketches are great. I'm glad you did one of Skip. Thanks a lot just what I needed. That's all for a while though." He handed her the envelope. "Maybe in a month's time I might need some more. Thanks again."

Rowan left deciding to walk Skip in the woods until dusk. She was still worrying what to do about Bill. Her father had upset her but she wasn't going to be bullied into anything. She walked much further than usual, the sun beginning to go down although it was still very warm, her nights had been restless and she was tired. Skip was still frisky so she tied him to a young sapling and sat under a nearby tree eating a few wild strawberries she had found on a sunny bank. Skip threw himself around for a while whining then lay with his head on his paws watching her. She wished she had a boyfriend then perhaps Bill would lose interest. She dozed for a while until a low growl and a sharp bark alerted her. Opening her eyes she was dismayed to see Bill walking through the trees towards her. She jumped up to get Skip but Bill was on her holding her tight in his arms, raining wet kisses on her face and neck. She shuddered and struggled.

"Let go of me." Trying to kick at his legs she found herself on the ground and he was lay on top of her. She screamed, his hand closed over her mouth.

"No My Pretty, there's no need to struggle now. We are good as engaged and that means we can love properly." She bit his hand; with an oath he slapped her face. Skip was going mad barking and straining to get to Rowan but the leash held firm. "That damn dog. I wish I'd brought my gun to shut him up. I told you to get rid."

With one hand he held both of hers above her head, he was heavy and strong and she was unable to move. With his other hand he began tugging at her clothes.

"We'll settle this now. You'll be spoilt for all but me, maybe a little one will come along and we'll have to get married quickly. I think we will any road."

He began tearing her blouse and freeing her breasts began sucking them first one then the other. She screamed again. He smacked her hard across the mouth. Her head throbbed and she thought she would faint. Breathing heavily he tugged again at her skirt pulling it up to her waist. As he released her hands to lift her skirt she twisted her hands in his hair but he didn't appear to feel it. She could feel the hardness of him as he sought entry. Suddenly he was seized from behind and flung across the clearing. Shocked, shaking and weeping with blood pouring from her lip, Rowan couldn't make out what was happening or who had grabbed Bill off her. Sounds of fighting and Skip's frenzied banking brought her to consciousness. The noise of crashing in the undergrowth came to her with the sounds of grunts and blows. The pain in her head and mouth kept her huddled on the ground searching for a handkerchief and trying to pull her torn blouse together. Suddenly there was silence. She tried to stand and failed, crawling over to Skip she sat with her arms around him as he whined and licked any part of he could reach. The sound of someone crashing through the bushes made her struggle to rise and untie Skip's lead. She was about to release him when she saw it was Jack staggering as he walked. He had a cut lip and a heavy blow to his face but he came to her and put an arm around her.

"Don't worry he's gone home to wash his bloody nose and bind up his sore ribs. He won't be about for a while. Can you walk as far as my cottage or shall I carry you?"

"I'm alright I think but I can't stop shaking."

"He didn't do what he wanted did he? Are you sure you're alright?"

"Yes I'm alright, I'm fine." She said again. He touched a finger to her red swollen cheeks "Not fine" he said "But safe. Thank God." They walked slowly his arm around Rowan without which she doubted she could have walked at all. Skip to her amazement, quiet at her side, he had not barked or growled at Jack; in fact Jack had bent down and stroked him.

"You would have seen him off wouldn't you boy if you could have?" Skip wagged his tail. Rowan was surprised to see how warm and comfortable the cottage was. A small fire burned in the range where a kettle was soon boiling. A cup of sweet tea was drunk in silence while Rowan rested in the big chair Skip at her feet. She looked up at Jack who was leaning against the mantel piece looking down at her, his eyes resting on her pale face. Her eyes were huge, marks of the slaps showing livid on her cheeks and swollen lips.

"Thank you so much. I don't know what I would have done if you hadn't been there. I'll be afraid to walk in the woods now in spite of Skip. How did you find me?"

Jack laughed. "Your mad dog. I was coming from the lake and thought I heard a scream. It didn't sound like a vixen not in daylight then I heard the dog, boy can he bark? He must have a sore throat by now." He bent down to give the dog a pat on the head and fetched a dish to give him a drink of tea. He brought a basin, warm water and a towel. "Better bather your face then it won't hurt so much. Do you want me to do it for you?"

"Thank you but I can manage. You are Tom Penry aren't you? Why call yourself – Jack and hide? You have a sister in the village and there's Joe and Tilly who would love to see you. What's the matter?"

Jack's face froze. "I can't answer that. Come, I must take you home. Don't be afraid to walk in the woods. You have your dog and I don't have anything better to do than keep an eye out for you. I won't stalk you or spy on you I'll just be about somewhere. I must cut and stack logs for winter so I'll be around. Just shout if you are worried."

"Thank you so much." Rowan was now beginning to feel weepy and needed to get home. Jack walked with her to the top of the track that led to the house. As she turned to go he touched her arm.

"Don't mention me to anyone please. I'll deal with things in time and in my own way. Oh! When you get in put some amica or cucumber on your face or bathe it in elder flowers, there are plenty about just now it will stop the bruising an tell your father about Bill whatever his name is?" He turned away.

"Oh! I'm sorry I should have tended your injuries." She was filled with remorse.

"Don't worry. I can pick elder too." He disappeared into the soft dusk.

Chapter 9

The sun was very hot for the time of year and everything was wilting in the heat. Soft white clouds drifted occasionally across the sky but there was no sign of rain. A breeze blew every now and then but was gone before it was enjoyed. Janet watered her drooping flowers, she didn't want to go in and tackle house work but she must and she'd thought she heard the phone. Reluctantly she rolled up the hosepipe and walked towards the house. To her surprise someone was waiting on the terrace, coming closer she recognised Ruth, Tom's wife with a small boy at her side.

"Hello, I didn't see you arrive and who is this with you?"

"I'm sorry Janet, to turn up without warning but I wanted you to meet Peter. This is your Aunty Janet, Peter, that I told you about."

The little boy was so like Tom it was uncanny. He shyly held out his hand although he was so small. Janet took it solemnly her throat full then pulled him close in a hug. "How lovely to see you and your mum, come in and have a cold drink. You'll stay to lunch won't you?"

"Actually Janet, I was wondering if you could put us up for a night. I need to talk to you and I am determined to see if that man in the cottage is Tom or not. I should have written but I wasn't sure what to do. I wrote to the army and waited for them to reply before I could do anything, it is certain that he was in hospital in Portsmouth but ran away from there, they lost track of him after he caught a train to Cornwall. He must be down here somewhere and I want to be sure that man isn't him. I had to bring Peter because I didn't know when I would be back. Do you mind Jan?"

"Of course I don't. I'm delighted to see you both. I wanted to find out more about that man but Matt has been so busy I couldn't leave him with the children as well but we must do something. We will have to go and find out once and for all."

After lunch the boys took Peter to play hide and seek in the shrubbery with their dog Gyp. By the squeals, shouts and barks all three were enjoying it. Janet and Ruth sat on the terrace and she began to tell Jan how she met Tom in Portsmouth before he was shipped out to France. They fell in love and married very quickly just before he left. Ruth's parents were angry and forbade them the house. They had been desperate for her to marry their local vicar's son. Because Ruth had inherited money from her Godmother that had been held in trust until she reached twenty-one that they had been able to rent a flat; here Ruth admitted she was five years older than Tom which was another fact that her parents disapproved of, "We wanted to tell you and Amy but we had so little time together and Tom meant to come and see you before he left but the time ran out and suddenly he was gone. He told me to write but like an idiot I lost the address."

"I know all about that," Janet told her of losing the address that she had been given by Meg the woman that had taken care of them when they were ill on their journey from Devon to Cornwall. "It had everything on that paper, the address of the woman we were going to work for. She had jobs lined up for us and all but I lost it I don't know how but I know just how you feel."

"I'm sorry Jan, then just after he left I found out I was pregnant, I didn't know what to do and my parent still wouldn't have anything to do with me. Tom had money sent to me but suddenly it stopped. Then I was lucky enough to find a job as a live-in housekeeper to an old lady who seemed to want to play with the baby occasionally. I have begged time off now to look for Tom but she is very frail and it just so happened that her cousin is staying at the moment but I mustn't be away too long."

"Oh! My dear I wish we had known, you and Peter could have come here. Perhaps we can sort something out if we can find Tom."

That evening talking with Matt they decided. Janet and Ruth should go to Indian Queens together. Janet would be able to see if Amy was coping and Ruth would take Peter to the cottage to see if the child would influence whoever was there to speak to them but Matt insisted that they ask Joe Treggoran to go with them. Janet persuaded Ruth to stay a day or two with them while she sent messages to Amy and Joe.

It was a strange sort of day when they left, the sky was a funny green-blue colour and clouds were building. A small wind kept whipping up and dying again, the atmosphere hot and thundery. Matt said there would be rain before long as the trees were showing the backs of their leaves. He waved them off on an early train and hoped they would arrive before the storm broke. Their journey however was pleasant although hot and by noon they were comfortably replete in the dining room of the Hen and Chicks where they had to wait for a bus to Indian Queens. Ruth and Peter dropped off at the entrance to the wood where it was only a short walk to Joe's house. They wouldn't be going to the cottage until the following day hoping Tom might be in if they left early enough. Janet continued to the village where she alighted crossing the road to Church cottage. It was very quiet. She hoped it was not a repetition of last time. Amy opened the door and hugged her sister.

"Hello Jan, it's lovely to have you come and stay with me for a bit. Come and see how Tommy had grown." They chattered as Amy made tea and carried Janet's bag upstairs while Janet grabbed Tommy to have a cuddle. She noticed the cottage was clean and tidy.

"Where are Ricky and Cissie." She asked as Amy came downstairs.

"They are with Joyce she has taken them to the post office on the promise of sweets. Thank you for finding her she is a treasure. Very hard working and doesn't leave me much to do except see to the children and the cooking."

"Glad to hear it" it looked to Janet as if Mrs Taylor or Joyce as they all now called her rather spoilt Amy and ran he household which wasn't quite Jan had meant by helping out. Amy was young and strong and Joyce elderly.

"Don't take advantage will you, Amy? You can cope you know."

"I know but she enjoys doing it all, when I help she says leave it, so I do. Treadle and Taylor we sound like a firm of solicitors."

They laughed and spent the next hour catching up on family news until Joyce came back with the children and

Violet and William came from school. In the general melee Joyce was persuaded to have a few days off while Janet was staying. Sep was going to be late as he had some work in the village to finish for the shop which was having alterations done. Amy fed the children then sent the older ones out to play while Janet put the younger ones to bed. As she came down stairs she had an idea, calling Amy in from the garden, she made them both tea.

"I've had an idea. You are a good cook Amy you used to do it when I wasn't well at the cottage. Why don't you take it up again? You could ask at the inn and the village shop and there's a good bus service now into St Austell to the market and Madeline's. Go in and see her she must get short sometimes. She can't go blackberry picking remember." They laughed together recalling the old days.

"It's a great idea but I'm not as good a cook as you are."

"Practice makes perfect." retorted Janet smugly.

"Well it's certainly worth a thought. I could go in and chat to Madseline. Thanks Jan I would certainly like to try. I'll have to ask Sep about it but I'm sure he'll agree; anything to keep me home." With a sly look at Janet who shook a warning finger.

Their talk turned to Tom. Amy thought she had caught a glimpse of the man from the cottage getting on the bus but was not close enough to be sure if it might be him.

"We'll know tomorrow if Ruth manages to catch him and you'll meet Peter Tom's son. He's so like him at that age it will make you cry."

"I can't wait neither can the children, Will and Violet can remember him but not very well". She rose to look through the window as the children ran in.

"This wind is much worse, don't any of you go out again, it's really bad out there now. I don't know what Ruth will do tomorrow if it's like this. I never liked those woods when there was a high wind and this one's like a hurricane you remember trees coming down when we were there. I hope Sep's alright, he was working on the roof but they'll have more slates off tomorrow I don't see the point."

At the moment Sep was almost blown through the door.

"Hello Janet. Good to see you. Don't even think about going into the woods while it's like this I had a job to stay on my feet let alone a ladder". While Amy cooked Sep's tea, Janet read stories to the children and put them to bed before settling for a chat with some homemade wine courtesy of Joyce. The storm was considerably worse with rain lashing the windows. If it hadn't improved by morning, there would certainly be no walk to the cottage.

Chapter 10

The storm gathered momentum in the night. Heavy rain lashed the forest like a monsoon. Howling wind kept everyone awake while thunder crashed, lightning forked through the trees and into the windows. Frightened children rushed crying into parents and even they were worried for their roofs and sheds. Joe went downstairs to make tea for everyone and attempted to see if the chickens and his garden shed was safe but the violence of the rain and strength of the wind wouldn't let him further than the porch, he gave up and returned to his bed. Ruth had seen many a bad storm over the coast but never one as sever and long lasting as this. Peter curled close in her arms and she sang to him softly until he slept again. She prayed she would find his father the next day but when morning came the wind still howled through the trees although the thunder had drifted off and the rain stopped. Tilly and Joe begged her not to attempt to go to the cottage but Ruth was adamant that it had to be today as she had to be back at work in two days.

"I don't want to go back, Mummy, I want to stay here." They all laughed at his serious little face. "I'm sorry darling but mummy has to go to work. We must go home tomorrow."

"May be the wind will have died down by tomorrow. Why don't you wait lass? Tid'ln safe in the woods and there'll be trees down for sure. That storm will have loosened the roots of others. Tid'ln safe; tell her Joe. The Penry's wouldn't go out in a bad storm they was always careful."

"I must try today I've only got until tomorrow." They set off against Joe's better judgement.

"Why don't I just go up and have another try with 'im?"

"No thank you Joe. It's Peter who might do the trick and seeing me face to face. I'll be glad of your company but I must do this" Joe grumbling fitted her out with wellies while Tilly wrapped Peter up warmly.

The sky had lightened but the wind was still at gale force and battered them as they walked. The ground was sodden and they were glad of their boots.

The road seemed long and being held back with the wind made it worse. Several trees had been uprooted and branches and debris littered the track.

As they approached what Joe called the street where the track ran between two rows of derelict houses; Peter wanted to run ahead but Joe caught his hand.

"It's too dangerous to go looking around now. We'll come back another day when the sun's shining". He swung Peter up onto his shoulders.

The wind seemed less fierce as they walked the street but as they passed a tall house which although a ruin, had its chimney still standing there was a loud cracking noise as a tree fell across it catching the chimney as it fell. Joe was slightly ahead of Ruth jogging Peter as he walked but Ruth stopped to glance up at the building; at that instant the chimney fell hitting her in the chest, with a cry she fell backwards the stones landing in a pile on her body. Joe shouted swinging Peter to the ground and hiding his face in his coat. The stones were massive and he knew already there was nothing he could do. Picking up the screaming child he raced for the cottage shouting all the while. Jack taken by surprise found himself at the door.

"Your wife – "gasped Joe fighting to get his breath while keeping hold of the screaming child.

"What wife? What are you talking about?"

"Ruth, man, you know Ruth, back down there on the path. Go to her but be careful more might come down. I'm going for help. This is your son Peter; I'll take him back to Tilly then run on to the village."

Jack turning ever paler and still disbelieving began to walk down the track, Joe hurrying after him as fast as he could with Peter struggling in his arms, saw Jack begin to run. There was no other way than to pass the scene again. With super human strength Jack had moved some of the stones from Ruth's upper body and was sat on the ground with her head in his lap cradling it and crying.

"Ruthie, Ruthie, Why did you come? I didn't mean to desert you. It should never have happened. I'm so sorry but I wasn't fit." Joe ran on the child growing heavier by the minuet, Peter sobbing all the while and begging to get down. Reaching the cottage Joe kicked the door open shouting for Tilly, as she came running he thrust Peter into her arms.

"No time to talk, there's been an accident Ruth is hurt bad. Don't let the boy out of your sight. Give him hot sweet tea and a drop of brandy in it he needs to sleep; he's seen too much. Emily you see to it, help your mother, I'll be back as quick as I can." He was gone. Tilly gathered the hysterical child in her arms, locked the door and stripped off his boots and outer clothing. He tried to refuse the tea when Emily brought it but Tilly made him swallow most of it then wrapping him in the big blanket off the settle rocked him crooning softly. Gradually as the sobs grew less he turned his head into her breast and fell asleep. After a while she laid him down on the settle still wrapped, placing a chair to stop him rolling off. Emily looked tearfully at her mother. "Do you think she will be alright?"

"I don't know what's happened Em. We must wait and see. Get the kettle on and hot water bottles out, we don't know what we'll need. Your father will be in shock as well, build up the fire while I make sandwiches in case they are needed quick."

Presently the sound of an ambulance and several other vehicles were heard rushing through the wood. Tilly with a terrible sense of foreboding suddenly remembered Janet and Amy. "Emily love, wrap up warm and run to the village and fetch the girls from Amy's. They must be here. Don't worry about the jobs I'll see to them, just be as quick as you can and take care it's still very windy."

"Shall I bring anything fom the shop on my way back?"

"We could use another loaf and some cheese. We've plenty in otherwise. Be quick now."

"Sometime later Joe brought Jack back with him. He was in deep shock and couldn't stop shaking. Tilly gave them sweet tea well laced with brandy. The doctor who had been summoned called in leaving some tablets for him and he was soon fast asleep in Martin's bed but not for long, he woke as Janet and Amy white faced came running up the lane.

"Oh! You poor lovers." Tilly flung her arms around them as Jack came down the stairs to hug his sisters and cry in their arms. The years they had thought him dead, the shock of knowing that he wasn't, the joy of having him safe at last and the knowledge of the terrible tragedy that they had to face together rendered them incoherent, they could only cling together and weep. Joe couldn't believe the solitary recluse had gone. Tom Penry had come home. The bright blue eyes were clear but unbearably sad his face haggard with grief.

I didn't know Jan, honestly I didn't know. I had forgotten all about her; how could I have been so cruel?"

"You have been to the most horrible war and you have been ill, maybe you are being too hard on yourself and carrying too much sorrow. Would it help you to talk about it if you can bear to that is?" Joe rubbed his hand over his graying hair. "I will always feel guilty that I couldn't go but I had rheumatic fever quite badly as a child and they wouldn't let me but what you went through must have been horrific."

Tom nodded. "I can see now that it's wrecking my life. I couldn't speak to anyone but I seem to have woken up now and although I never wanted to see or speak to anyone, I think the time has come, Poor Ruth, she didn't deserve what I did to her. I'll never forgive myself."

"Did you know that you had a son, did you know about Peter?"

"Of course I didn't. She didn't say anything in the few letters that I got and after I was deeper into the war they stopped. Where is he?" They both looked around at the small boy struggling off the settle. Tom went quickly weeping hugged him to him."

"Are you really my Daddy?" Big blue eyes looked into identical ones.

"Yes and I've been waiting a long time to meet you."

"Where's Mummy? Is she coming back here?" Everyone gasped then held their breath. "No Son." Tom was firm but gentle. "She had to go to heaven, the angels needed her but she sent me back to look after you and tell you how much she loved you." The little boy buried his face in his father's chest. "I miss her, I want her"

"I know Son. Shall we miss her together?" Peter nodded. Everyone in the room struggled to hide their tears. There was a knock on the door. Tilly went to answer it wiping her eyes on her apron. One of the policemen who had been called to the scene stood there, his helmet under his arm.

"Sorry to disturb you Mrs Treggorran but we need someone at the hospital for a forma identification of the body."

"Shall I go for you Tom?" Joe laid a hand on Tom's shoulder. "You've been through enough today."

"No thanks Joe. I must stand up to my responsibilities, I've been sick long enough." He placed Peter on Janet's lap. "Take care of him until I get back. Please be good Son. I won't be long."

"I'm coming with you." Joe grabbed his jacket and one for Tom who had raced out of his cottage regardless of the rain which had started again.

Tom turned at the door. "Please stay all of you, when I come back I'll tell you what happened to me. I will only be able to say it once and then I never want to speak of it again. Will you all do that for me?"

Amy kissed him. "Of course we will. Go and see Ruth. We aren't going anywhere." She turned as Janet having given Peter to Tilly put her arms around her sister as they wept together.

Chapter 11

The wind had subsided and a pale sun peeped through the trees highlighting the damage. Rowan walking carefully through the forest carried cages of patients now well and opening the doors released a rabbit, a shrew and two pigeons. She wandered looking for any casualties of the storm until she came to the street and saw the falling stones with splashes of blood, the tracks of several vehicles and many feet. Her heart hammered in her chest running to Jack's cottage she hammered on the door but there was no one there. She saw the chickens were still shut in so she let them out and fed them. The door swung wide as she pushed it, checking there was no one around she closed and locked it, worrying now as Tom never left his door open and the key was still on the inside. Putting the key above the door and calling Skip who was showing far too much interest in the stones, she raced down the track as fast as she could, jumping fallen branches arriving at Joe's house out of breath and with a stitch in her side. She didn't get the chance to know as Emily spotted her through the window.

"Come in Lass, we've trouble here" Tilly came from where she was sitting with a small boy in her lap. As Rowan entered she saw Amy her eyes red from crying with her arms around another she took to be her sister. Tilly too had been crying.

"What ever happened? I don't want to intrude but are you alright?"

Emily put a cup of tea into her hand and they all started speaking at once. "Where's Jack?" She realised suddenly that he wasn't there and her heart sank then began to beat very fast. It was Janet that told her what had happened that Jack really was Tom Penry and at the hospital with Joe. Rowan's heart steadied its furious beating on realizing that it was not Tom or one of the children. "Is there anything I can do." She asked tentatively her usual shyness overcome with the seriousness of the event, her first instinct being to run off into the woods.

"Yes lass" Tilly spoke over the crying and talking. "Would it be a problem for you to go and fetch Will and Violet from school and take them to Joyce Taylor's? She has got the little ones and I know I'm putting on you but could you put this note through Sep's door for Amy? I know I'm asking a lot but we would be grateful."

"Of course I will, I'd be glad to do anything to help." For the first time she noticed the little white-faced boy with tear filled eyes.

"This is Tom's son, Peter. If he would go with you he would be better with the other children away from here." Rowan looked at him seeing the likeness and powerful feeling of love and pity came over her.

"Hello Peter. Would you like to come with me and meet the children from school? We could go to the shop and buy some sweets and then you could meet some of my animals. My dog Skip is outside he would like to meet you too."

Peter looked at her a long moment seeing the big brown eyes full of love and listened to her soft voice. To everyone's amazement he slowly walked over to her and took her hand.

"Daddy's gone to see Mummy but he'll be back soon. I may as well." He smiled at her and his old fashioned speech shook her heart. They collected Will and Violet from school taking then to Joyce who when told well out of the children's hearing was horrified to hear what had happened. She soon had the children around the table with biscuits and lemonade.

"Tell Amy not to worry about them. I'll soon settle them with some drawing and later give them their tea. Poor Tom, I did wonder when I heard a man was at the cottage if it would be him. The girls have had such a shock one way and another. Give them my love. I'll take the children back when their father's home."

Rowan didn't leave Peter she took him home to her dispensary where she allowed him to feed a grey squirrel which had a damaged paw and some baby rabbits, a crow with a broken wing and Skip who now wanted his dinner. Peter was much happier seeing to all these with a thousand questions for Rowan. Later she took him in to her mother and Aunt Jean shocked at the tragedy took him under their wing taking him to feed Ned and give him his bath. Peter wanted a bath too so Dora let him some fun in the water before supper after which he fell asleep in a cot next to Ned.

Rowan didn't quite know what to do. She didn't like to go back to Joe's so she slipped into the woods to see if there were any casualties of the storm. It was with surprise that she saw Tom looking at the pile of stones that had killed Ruth.

He didn't see Rowan until she stood by his side. He turned to her his eyes full of tears.

"I didn't remember about her, why? I don't understand that and I can't forgive myself for that."

"You haven't been yourself." Rowan answered quietly.

"I know but it doesn't make any easier to bear." He dashed a hand across his eyes.

"Are you going to talk to your sisters? I know it's nothing to do with me but they must all be suffering one way or another."

"Yes I am going to tell them all that's been going on in my head and why. Would you come down with me? I am only going to tell it once and never speak of it again."

"Only if you want me to and they won't mind."

"Yes I do want you to whatever they say. It's you that has partly made it possible for me to do so by being the quiet fey person you are. You would never be part of any nightmare I can talk to you and you rest my soul. Please Rowan hear my story although you may never want to see me again when you have heard it."

Rowan remained silent but to his amazement slipped her small hand into his and held tight; thus hand in hand they walked slowly to Joe's cottage. The little house looked full to bursting. Martin and Sammy were home from work and Sep had just joined them. Janet had made tea Tilly had cut a mountain of sandwiches although no one seemed very hungry. Tom shook his head when offered and looked more than likely to run away but with Rowan's hand firmly grasping his he sat down and accepted a cup of tea which Joe fortified with a shot of whisky. Everyone found somewhere to sit as hesitatingly Tom began his tale.

Chapter 12

As I said before I shall only tell this once and I never ever want to hear a word about it again or have it referred to in any way.

When I was first sent to France it was an adventure and a great moral booster going with your mates to fight for your country and defeat the enemy. We all expected to return covered in glory. Our first skirmishes were like that, we all got promoted for our small acts of heroism. I hadn't been over there for more than six months before I was made a Captain for several incidents that I won't go into now. I don't even want to think about them because we thought that's what it's all about saving your men's lives and leading platoons here and there. We evacuated a few villages and fed a few more and thought we were brave and heroic when people in the streets cheered us on. It was easy putting up with the filth and the dirt, while we buried a few bodies and relieved a few villages because we were young and full of adventure doing our duty.

We weren't to know how long the war was going to last or how bad it was going to get. We kept pressing on, it took more and more out of us physically and did more and more damage mentally without us realising it. As we came to villages and towns full of people dying, begging us for food or asking us to bury their dead and the soldiers, French, German and other nationalities that had died fighting there as well, we became harder in some ways and more confused mentally. Confusion as to who was right or wrong. Many of the soldiers were mere boys and although enemies once they were dead there was no difference. I led a platoon of men into the battle of Ypres and never though it could get any worse than that. Then came the second battle, then the third between June and November 1917. We were in a village called Dichebrushe a ruined village south of Ypres approximately five miles behind the line. On the 30th of July, the day before the third battle began we moved to a spot behind Hill 60. We were three weeks with no protection from the elements other than canvas bivouacs, these were canvas sheets slung over one pole and pegged down. We crawled in on all fours eight men to a tent with a large assortment of other creatures following us in. I had never seen rats so big, like pet cats they followed us in and the lice and fleas were the least of our problems. When the guns started up, it felt like someone banging your head with a brick.

During five months of fighting for Passchendaele our company worked on the roads advancing as our line advanced while the Germans bombarded us day and night. When craters formed in the road we were sent with picks and shovels to repair them with anything we could find, stone, shells, broken guns and dead horses. When all was covered over the army moved on. The weather was atrocious; they said it was the heaviest rainfall for thirty years coming in the onset of winter we floundered deep in mud. We ate it, slept in it, some drowned in the shell holes full of water, they were deep and if you slipped and there was no one near to pull you out you drowned.

Then we heard that part of our division was being sent to Italy so we had far less men to protect the ridge when we were ordered to advance through a narrow pass. We were depleted in men, weary, drowning in mud but German reserves were released from the Eastern front and poured onto the ridge. To aid their defense they made full use of mustard gas which resulted in chemical burns. We heard that we had something like 310,000 casualties but we didn't feel anything about it, we were permanently numb".

There was a horrified gasp from the room, all of whom had been sitting in silence, Amy quietly weeping. Joe poured Tom another measure of whisky then without speaking took his place back on the floor where he sat with his boys and Sep.

After a minuet Tom continued. "The battle lasted for days. There was a continuous roar consuming all other sounds. Even violent explosions close by were undistinguishable, everything was one loud roar. It felt as if we were in the middle of one enormous volcano. We kept quiet as the big guns fought it out and trusted to luck. It felt like being in prison, too dangerous to get out, too dangerous for anyone to approach us. All around flew stones, shells, shrapnel, bullets, mud and earth; if any of them hit you, you would be crippled or dead. Many dugouts were hit and collapsed; when a lull came we all rushed to get our comrades out digging deep into earth, stones and water, some we rescued, many were dead, many screaming with injuries that our few medics were mostly unable to deal with. The stench was appalling except after the first few weeks we couldn't smell properly only the stench that invaded our clothes and hair.

The worst was to come when we were ordered onto the ridge. The German army was all around us and the slaughter began. I won't go into technical details but we never stood a chance; bodies collapsed on top of bodies burying men alive. How long it went on I don't know, all I can remember three of us crawling and fighting our way from under a mass of bodies dead and dying, several we shot ourselves so badly injured were they, screaming in agony with half a head and limbs missing, we couldn't leave them like it.

As we crawled we came upon bodies from previous battles rotting corpses alive with blue bottles and rats. Heaps of bones were sticking out of the ground. What happened to the two with me I don't know we got separated somehow, I crawled on too weak to stand, desperate for water, the pain in my head making me oblivious to other sounds. I could still hear the guns but that is all I could hear, they filled my head. Then I fell into some stinking shell hole and knew no more. When I finally came to I was in hospital clean and comfortable my leg and arm bandaged so I must have been injured somehow I couldn't feel a thing only dull aches and a pain in my head. I could still hear the guns though. I must have been there a while; I was conscious of being fed something and being cleansed, how long I don't know as I was out of it most of the time. When I did surface properly I couldn't bear to stay there because the worst of all things happened, everyone I looked at became gaunt and bloodied almost like skeletons. I felt as if I was dead and so were they so I just got up one night found some clothes in my locker, don't think they were mine not uniform anyway and my greatcoat on a chair. I'm ashamed to say I stole money from jackets hung on pegs in the passage, caught a train and came to the cottage, I remembered praying that no one was living in it. Someone at the hospital had told me the war was over but it didn't mean a thing.

I know who I was and where I was but everyone looked as if they were dead and I couldn't bear to see any of you looking like that, it would have sent me over the edge; if I wasn't already. I didn't remember about Ruth at all, they told me at the hospital that someone was asking about me but I was afraid to see who it was because they would have that I had a wife and didn't know about my son, she never told me or she did I never received those letters. Where is he by the way?"

"He's with my mother and fast asleep." Rowan replied her eyes full of tears.

Tom tried to speak and held out trembling hands and burst into tears. Janet flew to him gathering him in her arms. Emily held on to Rowan too shocked to speak. Tilly's boys and Sep hid their faces in their folded arms. Joe came from the kitchen with mugs of strong tea and the whisky bottle.

A while later Rowan got up to leave. "I must go feed my animals and see to your son. Thank you all for having me."

Tom rose to his feet his eyes bloodshot but at peace. "Forgive me everyone for unloading on you but I must see to my own son and go back to the cottage. As I said I never want to speak of it again but I feel as if much of the burden has gone. I see you as you really are and love you all. I'm missing Old Len but feel sure he would have listened too and understood. I haven't spoken so much for the last year; most of this is thanks to Rowan here who was able to talk to me and I found that I could speak to her and just see a normal beautiful face. Now you are all welcome at the cottage anytime but I won't be staying long, its magic has been destroyed by poor Ruth's death and I shall have to move on very soon."

There were cries of dismay from his sisters. Joe clasped his hand. "I understand that Tom. We'll miss you but you'll always be welcome here you know that." Tom gave him a hug. "I'll let you know what I decide." He turned to hug Janet and Amy.

"Don't get upset you two. I intend to spend a week or two getting to know your families, I want to see Madseline and 'Brambles' I'll let you know when I am ready to go don't fret."

"Do you want to come back with me? Janet asked hopefully. "I have to go home tomorrow."

"I can't for a while Janet. I'll settle things here first and after the funeral I'll stay with Amy and Sep for a bit but you will be back for Ruth's funeral. I'll let you know when." She kissed him again. "Of course I will. Keep well now and stay that way."

"I'll try." He hugged his sisters again and followed Rowan outside catching her hand as he closed the gate.

"I'd better come and get my son but I don't know if he will come home with me. Maybe he would be better with Tilly or Amy." When they reached the Berryman's, they found Peter sat with Jed, Dora and Aunty Jean eating chicken casserole and plum duff. He seemed very much recovered. Dora took Tom on one side.

"He's coming out of shock but you'll have to be careful. I can't see him going to your cottage the image is too fresh and he's far from steady yet. In a day or two he's going to miss her a lot more."

Tom rubbed his chin thoughtfully. "What do you suggest?"

"If he's happy to stay here we'd love to have him as long as you can spend time with him and get to know each other."

"I'll talk to him and see." Tom shook hands with Jed and Jean then lifting his son down from the table took him outside to play ball for a while. Afterwards he bathed him and put him to bed in Ned's room reading him a story from Rowan's collection of childhood books. Just before he left him for the night he asked him if he would like to stay with Rowan and Ned for a while.

"Yes I like it here they've got kittens and rabbits and birds in Rowan's shed and Skip likes me he licks me but will you come to see me? Will Mummy know where I am?" Tom blinked away his tears. "Of course she does, she always knows where you are and lovers you very much. Go to sleep now and I will see you tomorrow. Rowan will take care of you tonight." He kissed his little son as he cuddled down to sleep, Rowan's old teddy bear under his arm.

Chapter 13

Rowan had been very quiet after they left Tilly's house. She had let Tom put Peter to bed and went to her dispensary where Tom found her. He talked to her for a while about her patients, very interested in what she did.

"You make a great veterinary nurse." He told her. Is that what you want to do with your life?"

"I don't know." She answered slowly. She had been more disturbed than she realised when Tom told his story and then said that he was going away. She longed to ask for how long but didn't have the courage. Retreating into her shell she just quietly fed her patients. Tom was puzzled by her silence, perhaps she didn't want anything to do with him after hearing his awful tale. "Peter is staying here for the time being. I will be down each day to spend time and get to know him, more importantly he will come to know me. You'll be here won't you?" He asked anxiously. "Are you worried about that man still, afraid to walk in the woods?"

"Yes a little nervous." Rowan replied. Tom looked at her a moment before he said slowly. "I have an idea. How about I come to see Peter and we both take him through the forest; not to my cottage." He hastened to add. "To the lake and the village, perhaps teach him to fish, you could show him the things you know about. He's too young for school but very bright."

Rowan smiled. "That would be great. I could teach him a little, letters and numbers.

"I could get him to draw as well." She explained about her illustrations.

"That would be wonderful. When I go to stay with my sisters he will have his cousins to play with" Tom took both her hands and kissed her cheek. "Thank you for being so kind and caring and helping me through this, I am not right yet but much better."

"It's alright. I'm not very good with people but you were alone. I thought I remembered you but wasn't sure and you were shy too and that helped."

Tom squeezed her hands. "I think we may be good for each other then." He left her blushing slightly stunned by what he was implying. She would miss him when he left but she had the days in the forest with him and Peter to look forward to. She began to hum to herself as she cleaned the empty cages in readiness for any new tenants.

Meanwhile Janet and Amy had returned to Amy's cottage with Sep who collected the children from Joyce. They had to answer a few questions diplomatically. They all slept badly, their heads filled with the horror of Tom's story and what he had been through. To the two girls Jake's murder on their journey to Cornwall had seemed at the time the most terrible think in the word. Now it seemed tamed and had lost its nightmare quality in the horrors of the First World War. They awoke heavy eyed and weary although they were over the moon at Tom's recovery. They decided to go and see Madseline to tell her about Tom and that he soon would be visiting her. They would meet her husband again also named Peter and their baby Mark.

Madseline had taken over 'Brambles' after Janet had married Matt Jordon. It was still a flourishing cake shop and café. Polly still managed the cake shop and was now engaged to the local policeman. As Maddy was expecting a second baby she was advertising for someone to manage the café. She did employ two girls part time but needed someone more experienced. Maddy's husband Peter Knowles adored his wife and baby son but had little time to help in the business having his own butcher shop the other side of the town but as Maddy said with a laugh she never had to worry about the meat side of things.

Janet and Amy had a great time with Maddy catching up with the news and gossip. She was so excited that Tom was alive and couldn't wait to see him again although horrified at all he had been through and the loss of his wife in such a tragedy. She too had sad news. Her mother who had been such a lovely artist, hand painting pottery although wheelchair bound was now in a nursing home. Maddy had told Janet when it happened and Janet had intended to visit her this time, but as Maddy said with tears in her eyes there was no point as she had developed dementia and didn't even know her own daughter.

Apart from that they enjoyed the day with her sister and friend, talking about their pasts, gossiping about the town and delighting in baby Mark who was just beginning to walk.

"Don't get broody, Amy. I know you." Janet watched her sister playing with the little boy. Amy looked up her eyes bright. "I know but I always enjoy someone else's because I can hand them back. My own get me down sometimes but I love them all." Janet was silent she only hoped that Amy was settled now. She and Sep seemed closer lately with Mrs Taylor helping out and doing a bit babysitting for them occasionally.

Maddy laughed. "I expect I shall be the same when this next ones here. Now tell me all about Tom. I am so excited that he's back and getting better."

Later they took a turn around the town and visited Peter's shop where he joked and laughed with them then sent them home with a leg of lamb and a pound of mince to Amy's delight. "I'll be back for a turkey come Christmas." It was sad to see Janet onto the train home but she and Matt would be back for Ruth's funeral the following week; not an occasion they were looking forward to but must be done.

Meanwhile Rowan enjoyed looking after Tom's son and the days spent in the woods with them both were a delight to her. She found Tom a delightful companion and he seemed to know as much about the woods as she did. "Well I did grow up here." He replied when she asked him how he remembered it all. He took them to see the charcoal burners at work and they enjoyed a picnic the far side of the forest. He showed Rowan how to tickle trout but she didn't catch any. Peter was delighted to have two grown up playmates and happily took interest in all they did. He especially loved playing with Skip who would patiently pick up stick after stick when the little boys efforts to throw them for him merely landed almost on Peter's own feet.

They grew closer and a tingle passed between them when Tom caught her hand which happened more and more often. It seemed he held her a bit longer each time he helped over a stile or fallen tree. She who had never needed assistance with anything grew to expect with a feeling of excitement every contact with his warm hands and bronzed arms. He felt he was bathing in her big brown eyes and warm shy smile. He felt he had to say and do things to make the dimples come and go in her cheeks and keep those soft lips smiling. The nightmares had all but gone now but he couldn't wait to leave the cottage as the scene of Ruth's death was almost at his door. He loved the feeling which was growing every time he saw Rowan but knew that he had nothing to give her and that she deserved so much more. She in turn waited on his every move but was too shy to say or do anything to move forward. They both devoted themselves to Peter and the little boy blossomed under their care and only occasionally asked when his mother was coming home. He could almost always be distracted with the animals they saw in the woods and Skip's excited barks when he saw a rabbit or a squirrel.

The evening before the funeral they were later coming back with Peter, he had fallen asleep in Tom's arms and they idly walked chatting as they came, Tom stopped suddenly at the same moment that Rowan grabbed his arm. Ahead of them as they came to the edge of the wood, there was a sudden movement as a deer crossed the track from one side of the woodland to the other. It was gone swiftly but they both saw quite clearly it was pale in colour, as it crossed it hesitated only a second but enough for them to see it only had one horn, barely had they taken in what they were seeing it had gone, only a faint rustle as it disappeared.

"Do you believe it?" Rowan whispered clutching Tom's arm.

"I do now, I didn't when I saw it once before. I believed it was just an unusual colour and had an accident sometime but it didn't look like that tonight."

"I saw it once when I was about twelve and didn't tell anyone as I thought they would laugh at me but you've seen it too; it has to be right, hasn't it?"

"Well it is to us and that is all that counts." He put the sleeping boy in her arms as they came near to her door. As her arms were full with the child against his better judgement he kissed her lips before slipping away into the wood.

Chapter 14

The day of the funeral was a miserable day. From summer it had returned to winter. Wet and windy it was too reminiscent of the day the storm had taken Ruth's life. The trees loomed heavy with moisture, dripping onto the villagers as they made their way to the church, the mournful tolling of the bell adding to the depression of the day. Matt and Janet drove up a little late after seeing to their boys. Amy and Sep had gone to the Treggorrans to go with them for support. Amy couldn't stop crying and Tilly spoke to her sharply urging her to pull herself together for Tom's sake.

"If he turns up." muttered Sep darkly. "He may go into one of his panic attacks."

"Rowan is going to the cottage to come down with him." Joe replied. "It was arranged days ago. They are getting very close those two. It would be good for both of them if something came of it."

"Here they are now." Amy ran to her brother and hugged him. Rowan smiled at her shyly. Many of the villagers had turned out. The story that Jack Travers was Tom Penry had become knowledge and some who genuinely cared about the family that had once lived in the woods and many who were just curious all turned out to pay their respects. It was a difficult day. Peter and Madseline came also Mrs Taylor who was to take the little ones home with her. There was no one from the Hall but Jan expected that, although they would have heard of the accident they would have lost their concern over the Penry family. Lord Arlington having passed away the year before, Lady Jane now spent most of her time in Scotland with her elder son and his family. Sir Geoffrey spent most of his time, hunting, shooting and fishing according to the villagers leaving his wife and two daughters to amuse themselves. Janet didn't want to think about him and their brief love affair. She for one was glad they weren't here today.

"Come on everyone. Vicar's waiting. Let's go on with it. Ruth has waited long enough" Tom strode forward and everyone followed. It was soon over and they gathered at the graveside where many flowers were laid on the grass.

"What happened to her parents?" Tilly whispered to Janet. "They couldn't come according to Mr Thompkins." She nodded towards the solicitor who stood apart from the crowd at the graveside. "Apparently her mother's very ill and her father unforgiving 'though he wants to see Peter by all accounts.' That's up to Tom now."

They all returned to Joe's where Tilly laid a good spread but few villagers stayed. It was a relief when everyone had left and Tom took Janet to fetch Peter as he had decided to stay with her for a while, coming back to see Amy later. He had decided on this change of plan as he felt Amy's household was too noisy for himself and Peter, he felt they needed to settle down a while and he couldn't bear to be in the cottage a moment longer than necessary.

Rowan watched them depart with sad eyes and a heavy heart. She only had the few moments with Tom when he took her aside.

"I'm sorry to leave you like this but it's better for Peter and me to get away for a while. I'll be back in a couple of weeks and I would like you to think on something while I am away. When I come back I shall stay with Amy for a while then Peter and I will move away. There are too many memories here now, we need a fresh start. I know we haven't met long and haven't got to know each other well, we haven't had the chance also you are settled here with a family who would miss you but would you consider moving away with me?" He placed his finger on her lips as she began to speak. "Not now my love, wait until I'm back at Amy's and we will have time to talk properly. I promise I would take great care of you and Peter loves you. I will need some help with him as the authorities are not keen on a man looking after a child if he's not married also I shall have to find work. Please think on it while I am away that's all I ask." Before she could speak he kissed quickly on the lips then joining the others he was gone.

Rowan was speechless; tears starting to her eyes. She was confused and bewildered. Where were the walks in the woods and teaching Peter his letters all gone? There had been no further mention since the few days they had spent this last week. He hadn't said how he really felt, whether he cared for her. Did he think she would just tralpse off like a gypsy? Did he just want a housekeeper someone to look after his child? Was he looking for a mother for his son?

She called Skip and walked in the woods for a long time tears coursing down her cheeks. The dog sensed her unhappiness and kept to her side. She kept a wary eye and ears open for Bill but he had seemingly gone to ground lately. That was another thing. He had been so concerned about her walking alone in the woods. What about that? He had driven off without thought. Well she had survived without him before she could again. When her burst of anger passed, she realised she probably couldn't. She was in love with him.

Rowan was scared, scared of being used for a man's ends. She was naïve but still sure enough that she wanted love and marriage in that order. She was also mature enough to know that although she had fallen for Tom and his boy she would not go with him blindly without knowing how he felt about her. She knew that she was in love but was he?

She tried to immense herself in her little dispensary, as there were no patients at the moment she cleaned it out and whitewashed walls and ceilings cleaned all the cages disinfecting as she did so then made a bonfire of all the rubbish. She volunteered for more hours at the village surgery and was pleased when they accepted her offer of a spring clean there especially as they too were down on patients. She was even more pleased to receive a message from Ralph Conway telling her he was off to Italy for a month or two but if she would care to sketch some wolves coming out of the forest and a series of wild woodland flowers and post them to the enclosed address, he would be grateful. 'We can always work by post because I don't want to have anyone else as you do them so beautifully and you know how I like things done.' He enclosed a postal order to cover her work, postage and packing which was more than generous.

Rowan plucked up courage one day to approach Tom's cottage keeping her eyes averted from the 'street'. It was once again deserted and abandoned. Locked and boarded up with only a tiny window she could peer through. All the furniture was once again piled in the centre of the room and covered with the red rug. It looked as if Tom had never lived there. She turned away, the garden was bare and only some sticks and remnants of seed packets tied to them remained. Rowan felt the tears block her throat. Everything was so forlorn, deserted and lonely and Rowan who had never been depressed or lonely in her life couldn't bear it. She hurried down to Tilly to see if there was any news, she welcomed her with a warm hug and a cup of tea but Rowan could see she was busy turning her house out so she drank the tea quickly and went home. Her mother met her at the door baby Ned in her arms.

"There's a letter for you. It might be from Tom. Can't read the postmark" Dora turned back to the kitchen where her sister Jean was baking. Rowan's spirits rose and she raced upstairs to her room to read her letter.

My Darling Rowan,

Hope you are taking care of yourself. Keep Skip close always. I hate to tell you but I won't be back for a while as Matt has given me a job helping him and although I miss you very much, it's good to be away from the woods for a while. It won't be too long as I am healing more and more each day. Life is fine and Peter is enjoying being with his cousins. Jan spoils him but he is well and getting more and more cheerful. I miss you and our walks and talks. I shall take a weekend off just new and come to see you. We haven't had much time together, my little fawn but it will come right soon. Take great care and don't go too far in the forest.

Your Tom xx

Rowan didn't know whether to be happy or sad. He had written calling her darling and said he missed her. He had signed kisses but at the same time the two weeks he said he would be away now seemed forever and a weekend meant that he would be going back. Where did this leave her? She sighed, she would just have to wait and see. She pressed the letter in the book at her bed side and went down to share her news and play with Ned.

It was later that night that she was woken by a low growl from Skip who now slept by her head. Listening she could hear there was a horse outside, his feet moving restlessly on the cobbles, a door closed and she could hear a murmur of voices. Kneeling up at the window she peeped through the curtains. Her heart stopped. Bill Wilkins was shaking hands with her father before mounting and riding quietly away. There was something going on. She had trusted her father but when she had tried to tell him about Bill attacking her he had been first of all angry and said he would have a word with Bill but later told her she was getting upset about nothing. Yes Bill had been a bit too keen but he had apologised to Jed for frightening her and assured him that he would never hurt her. It was that fellow from the cottage had made the situation worse and interfered in what wasn't his business. She felt betrayed. How could the father she adored have let that snake in the grass into his house let alone shake hands with him. She knew her mother and aunt had long gone to bed or there would have been ructions. They both disliked him and after she had told them what happened and that Tom had rescued here, Dora had sworn she would not have him on the place and her and Jed had rowed about it. Her father refused to listen, swore that Bill was a good man, he had known him all his life. He had talked to Bill who had assured him that he had only tried to kiss her, the shy little thing that she was had panicked and that looney Jack or Tom or whatever he was called had made it much worse that it was filling her head with nonsense. He Bill wanted to marry her and keep her safe on his farm and he had convinced Jed that Rowan's roaming days were over and she had better come to terms with it.

Things had gone quiet since for weeks and now this; something was going to happen she could feel it and she wasn't safe. The further she went from here the better. She would love to go to Tom but what would it look like? Rowan was a little nervous of Janet. What if she thought Rowan was chasing him when he still wasn't fit to be worried? It just wouldn't be right. Maybe Tom would feel compromised and what if he didn't love her? No she couldn't possibly go to him; it wouldn't be right and put too many people in difficult positions. It would be no good going to Amy or Tilly. Bill or her father would be soon on the doorstop. She had to get right away. She tossed and turned all night worrying without a solution. If only she was twenty one but she wasn't. She fell into a doze around dawn and woke late. As she opened her eyes she knew where she wanted to go.

Chapter 15

Winter was coming early. The autumn had been a blaze of red, gold and bronze. The big storm had started the leaves falling now they carpeted the forest with a deep bed of brown. It was turning colder by the day and already a slight frost had touched the grass. The deer were coming slowly closer and Rowan enjoyed seeing them again. Through the winter she would feed hay she bought from a local farmer and already a herd was beginning to collect in the clearing. There was no sign of the pale one horned stag that both she and Tom had seen. She kept well way from the ruined village and Tom's cottage though sometimes she took Skip down to the lake always half hoping that Tom might be there. It was cold and glassy now with the sheen of ice.

Becoming more and more nervous by the day of going too far even with Skip, as Christmas drew near she made her plans, as soon as the year turned she would go. The Berryman's always celebrated a traditional Christmas, church in the morning followed by a huge Christmas dinner to which several relatives usually travelled to attend and stay the night. This year as Aunt Jean was already here it was only Jed's brother Nick and his wife and two daughters to arrive on Christmas Eve from Gloucester. Rowan was not over fond of Nick or his wife Maggie. They were noisy and she always felt uncomfortable with them. Their daughters were better. Miranda the eldest was pretty and friendly but being a town girl her main interests were clothes, make up, talk about boys and her friend Sophie. She had little interest in Rowan's activities. Her younger sister Susan was almost too interested following Rowan everywhere. The two days they stayed she never left her side, not minding the mud and ice, she just blindly went where Rowan went talking all the time about her school, the films she'd seen, her friends in Painswick where they lived and what subjects she was doing at school, also the endless questions about everything nearly drove Rowan wild. On returning from church on Christmas morning to her horror, Bill Wilkins was tying up his horse at their gate. Jed promptly invited him in to dinner ignoring Rowans distress and his wife's furious glare. Her Aunt Jean steered Rowan out into the kitchen and kept her busy until dinner was ready also moving her chair further down the table, beside her own where, Rowan found herself the focus of Susan's idolising eyes and Bill's possessive stare. Completely losing her appetite she pushed her food around her plate until the meal was over. Later in the afternoon presents were exchanged, everyone much amused at Ned's fascination with the wrapping paper rather that his toys. Rowan had received a small package and letter from Tom which she couldn't wait for the privacy of her room to open. She had managed to post a scarf she had knitted and a small sketch of deer grazing earlier in the week. With dismay she saw Bill was pushing a parcel along with the family's presents towards her. She tried to avoid it but once she had opened the others she was left with it on her lap with everyone watching. It turned out to be a pair of mittens made of rabbit skins. She thanked him and pushed them deep in her chair to be disposed of later. Alone at last in her room she opened Tom's letter.

'Hello! Little One.

Hope you are alright and enjoying your day. Thank you for the scarf I shall wear it all winter. The sketch I have framed and it stands on my bedside table. It is so full of memories and reminds me of you. Take care, my love. Hope to see you soon. Give Skip a hug.

Yours Tom xx

The little packet contained a St Christopher medal on a fine chain which she promptly put on under her clothes.

Two days later she went to visit Amy with sweets for the children. They all made her welcome showing her their presents and all taking at once. Amy gave her tea and Christmas cake.

"We've heard from Tom and he sent lovely gifts but he's not coming back for a while. He's helping Matt but they can't come up at the moment as they are too busy. Did you have a good Christmas?" They chattered for a while, the children taking their attention as each wanted to show her their gifts. Rowan rose to leave taking Amy on one side.

"Do you remember Meg the woman that helped you when you travelled down here?"

"Of course." Amy looked surprised. "We write to her regularly at least Jan does more than me; I'm sorry to say. We sent her gifts from the children. We hope to see her in the spring but she is getting on now and her nice is looking after her. Why do you ask?" Rowan hesitated as she didn't want to tell Amy about Bill.

"Tom talked a lot about her and her beautiful garden. I would like to write to her if you don't mind giving me her address." This seemed a pretty lame excuse to Rowan but Amy didn't seem to notice.

"Wait I'll get it for you. It would be lovely of you. Maybe you'll meet her some day or come with us." She hurried off returning with a letter. "It's on here, you might as well take it I have others."

Rowan thanked her hurrying off half afraid to look at the letter she was holding. It was probably the opposite direction to the one her Uncle would take on his way home, she had considered going back with them but it would take too much explaining also Uncle Nick had become very friendly with Bill over drinks at Christmas. To her great relief she saw that Meg lived not too far away; at least she would be able to make it under her own steam. It was not too far from Holsworthy but in an isolated country area. Rowan could take a train to Holsworthy then find a way to cross country to Meg's cottage. There was no time to write, she would just have to take a chance and if Meg couldn't or wouldn't take her in she would just have to find somewhere else, Maybe Meg could find Rowan lodgings with a neighbor.

Rowan was getting nervous of walking the woods she just knew Bill would make another move on her before long. He was calling on Jed more often lately. Her next call was on Tilly and Joe who welcomed her warmly thrusting tea and cake upon her almost before she sat down.

"How are you dear? Missing Tom I'll bet". Tilly was peeling potatoes for dinner. "He won't be back for a bit by the sounds of it. What a shame when yer had only just got to know each other too. Don't ee miss 'im?"

"Yes I do." Rowan admitted. "But I am going away to my cousins for a while." She hesitated, reluctant but tempted to tell Tilly about Bill. "Someone around here is getting too close for comfort and I need to be out of the way for a bit."

Tilly's brow darkened and her lips set in a thin line.

"Tiz alright, I know my girl. That there Bill Wilkins 'he's a bad 'un. Tom asked Joe to keep an eye out for you. Ter think yer father's encouraging him. He's no match for a shy young thing like you. Tiz a wife and a slave he's looking for to replace poor Martha. Terrible life she had with 'im womanising all over the place, leaving all the heavy work to her and her not well. What yer going to do lass, go to 'is sister's?"

"I can't, Bill will find me, my father will see to that. No I'm going up country to Meg who took them all in years ago. I only hope that she can take me in; any way I'll get a job until Tom comes back; if he wants me that is," She fingered the St Christopher she wore constantly.

"Oh! He'll want yer never fear that. You helped bring 'im to his senses. Why don't we write and tell 'im ter come back and look after you."

"Oh! No." Rowan jumped up. I'm not sure how he feels. I'll wait until he comes back. We'll see. "I came to ask Joe to do me a favour. Is he about?"

Tilly shrieked up the garden to where Joe was mending a hole in the hedge. It was bitterly cold he came in stamping his feet, his cheeks red, woolly hat pulled down to his eyes.

"Hello Rowan. What's up? Yes Tilly I could do with a cuppa and some of that cake. I reckon it's got to snow."

"Joe I need a favour, I'm going away for awhile but I'm worried about the deer. I've been feeding them with hay that

I buy from Fallow farm. It's a cheek I know but if I buy in a few bales could you feed them for me?"

"Of course I will. I'll pay for a few as well if it gets too low and Sammy will help me anyhow. He's fond of the deer. Don't worry. Who's looking after your little hospital and Skip?"

"Skip I'm taking with me. Bill will shoot him if he sees him about and the little animals are all gone except for a hedgehog and he's hibernating. I'll make sure that there is a hole so that he could get out of if he wakes before I'm back. Thank you both so much."

"What do yer parents think about yer going?" Tilly folder her arms.

"I haven't said yet. I'll leave a note for mother when I go; what she'll say to father I don't know but he mustn't know where I've gone. Thank you both again."

"Wait a minute." Tilly turned to the dresser. "Take this in case." She pressed two folded notes into Rowan's hand.

"I can't take this." Rowan gasped pushing them away.

"You go on. We can afford it now the boys are working and you might be desperate."

Rowan hugged her and Joe. "I'll pay you back I promise." Tilly hugged her harder. "Go on with yer. Take care of yerself and come back ter us soon. "Pity ye've missed Emily. She's gone shopping. She'll miss yer, we all will." They waved her off. She left tears in her eyes wondering if she was doing the right thing after all.

Chapter 16

Dora was worried, there was something going on with Rowan and she couldn't get her to talk. Ever evasive and secretive she just said when questioned that she was fine and promptly left the room. Jean did no better but said 'best leave her alone". Jean was more concerned about her sister.

"Don't fret so much about her. Rowan is a good girl and if Jed would only stop pushing her to that Bill Wilkins, she would be alright and a lot happier.

She's missing the Penry boy, that's half the problem, she'll settle down." Ned took their attention and no more was said. Later in their room Dora confronted Jed.

"Rowan is unhappy. She's missing Tom and you keep pushing Bill at her. He's too old, too rough, he's been married before and Rowan dislikes him. Look at the way he frightened her." Rowan hadn't told her mother other than Bill frightened her. She had told her father rather more but he didn't believe her.

"It was just Bill getting a bit carried away he only wanted to kiss her. She's too childish and too wrapped up in childish things. This business with injured animals and tramping the woods at all hours must stop. Scribbling those pictures for that artist fellow is doing no good either. There's no harm in Bill. When she comes to her senses she will there is more going for her with Bill than that of Penry boy; he's only just out of the army, no job, no prospects I doubt much money either, anyway he's gone and probably won't be back. Rowan's just going to get over him and see sense. She's too old to go messing in the woods. She needs to grow up."

Dora was angry but knew she was beaten Jed would never listen to her. Her heart bled for her daughter but there was nothing she could think of to stop it happening.

Rowan had puzzled how to tell her mother what she planned, Jed would soon have it out of her and be looking for her. After a sleepless night she penned a note saying she was going to stay with a friend of the Penry's for a while, not to worry about her, she would be writing later. She was fin but needed to get a way for a while, signed it with love and placed it on her bedroom mantelpiece. She filled a holdall with some clothes, her sketch pad and pens and a couple of books. In her backpack she had Skips food, bowl and a bottle of water, these she sneaked out and hid in the lane before going in for breakfast. Her train left at twelve o'clock. She quickly did her chores then said she was going shopping and might be a while, to her dismay she was then presented with a list for Ned and a few things for Aunt Jean. This was upsetting but there was nothing she could do.

Once in a town she collected her savings from the post office. It wasn't much but thanks to her recent payments from the vets, Ralph Conway and Tilly, it might be enough to keep her until she could find work. What she would do with Skip when she did hadn't entered her head. On buying her ticket she found she had to pay for Skip as well. Once the train left the station she enjoyed the journey. For

Rowan who had never travelled before it was a delight. The trees were turning colour, bronze and gold while the fields were still bright green except where farmers were harvesting corn, fields of gold and brown delighted her artist's eye. She promised herself she would paint them when she was settled. Skip slept at her feet not worrying where he was as long as he was with his mistress. Rowan knew she wasn't wise going to Meg without warning. If she couldn't take her in she would have to find somewhere she and Skip could sleep tonight but her senses seemed to have deserted her these last few days, only now she was beginning to worry. She missed Tom wishing she had gone to him instead but her father and Bill had mothered her so much she could barely think straight.

On arriving at the station she bought tea, a sandwich and some stale buns for Skip who soon demolished them. She made enquiries pleased to find there was a bus which would take her within two miles of Meg's cottage; after which she would have to walk the rest of the way. Rowan didn't mind walking but her holdall and backpack were heavy, the country strange and the late afternoon becoming colder, it would soon be dark. Coloured leaves swirled around her in the chilly wind. Her tried brain worried at the situation; what if Meg was away or was ill and gone to live with the niece, she was in trouble, not about sleeping out if she had to. The temperature was dropping; thankfully she had Skip to cuddle up to and protect her.

The way seemed long, strange ground always did, trying to hurry to reach her destination before dark she tripped and measured her length on the ground with an anxious Skip washing her face. Not hurt but shaken she got to her feet reassured Skip and walked on wishing Meg would come along in her cart as she had for Janet, Amy and Tom; she mustn't think about Tom, her steps quickened, Skip trotting along beside her.

"It was dusk as she approached what she hopefully believed to be the right cottage seeing thankfully a light in the window, making her way up an overgrowth path she knocked on the door.

"Who is it?" The voice was young, maybe it was the wrong cottage.

"Sorry to disturb you. Does a lady called Margaret Thornton live here? You won't have heard of me but I am a friend of Tom Penry. My name is Rowan Berryman. I've come from St Austell."

The door was slightly opened secured with a chain by a young woman holding a lamp "Can I help you"

"I've come to see Meg, is she in?"

"Yes she is but it's late and she's resting. Can I help?"

"I was hoping to speak to her and I need somewhere to stay tonight. My dog is friendly. I have come a long way." The girl turned away and spoke to someone in the room repeating Rowan's words. After a moment she came back and undid the chain.

My aunt says to come in but I don't know about the dog. We have two cats."

"I can't leave him but he's very docile unless someone attacks me. I promise that he won't even look at your cats." Rowan smiled. The girl laughed.

"It's alright. Madge has fled upstairs already and Kitty won't mind she is completely deaf and going blind. Come in." She pushed the door wider and took Rowan's bag. "Go through, Aunty is in the sitting room." Rowan kept Skip close as she timidly went in.

The room was very warm a log fire blazing up the chimney. Rowan's eyes were drawn immediately to a small figure wrapped in a long shawl sitting in a deep armchair, the tall lamp behind her gleaming on her silver hair, glasses perched on her nose and an open book lay on her knees.

"Who is it Ginny?" Her voice was surprisingly strong and clear.

"A young lady who says she is a friend of the Penry's Ginny's slightly raised voice inclined Rowan to think Meg may be rather deaf"

"Come closer, my dear. Don't worry about the dog he looks friendly enough and my cats are out of the way. Sit down and let me see you. A friend of the Penry children you say but they aren't children anymore; all grown up now. Ginny be a dear and make some tea, we'll have a cup before dinner and bring some water for the dog. You'll have come a long way and it's lovely to meet you. I understand I'm to call you Rowan, pretty name, I have a tree in my garden and your dog's name?" She paused at last for breath.

"His name is Skip and I'm sorry to bother you so late in the day, I should have written I'm sorry."

"It's quite alright a friend of the Penry's is always welcome." Rowan was now conscious of the strange lavender eyes regarding her steadily. An unusual colour and very piercing, Rowan thought 'no one would fool this lady' However her smile was very genuine and sweet. When Ginny entered with the tea and came into the light she was a very pretty girl, russet curls piled on her head and very big brown eyes. Her smile was warm and welcoming Rowan liked her on sight. She brought a dish of water for Skip and a handful of biscuits. He also liked her on sight, licking her hands as she bent to pat him, he took the biscuits gently and then licked her nose. Rowan drank the tea and wondered how to broach the reason for her visit. Meg drank her tea in silence then leaned back in her chair fixing her strange eyes on Rowan.

"I sense a special reason for this visit." She folder her shawl around her and waited. Rowan realised she had to be very straight with her and tell the whole story.

"I am sorry to come to you without asking but I had to get away somewhere that Father and Bill wouldn't know about. Tom told me so much about you and how you took them in and I didn't know of anyone else to go to. I'm sorry if it's an imposition. I will find a bed and breakfast somewhere. I'll have to find work quickly." She paused her eyes full tears filling her throat. She was tired, the journey had filled her with apprehension and it now seemed a very cheeky thing to come without permission. There was silence except for the crackling of the fire and Skip's lapping as he drank more water noisily. Meg had closed her eyes and Rowan thought she may have fallen asleep. Ginny watched her and waited. Meg suddenly opened her eyes and sat forward.

"You were right to come, child. That was no place for you, pushing you like that. It's not right in this day and age; it amounts to bullying. You need time to think. I need time to think so if Ginny will make us some dinner we may think much better afterwards"

Rowan offered to help but Ginny declined. "You are tired and I know where everything is, just rest and talk to Aunty Meg."

The dinner was stew with dumplings followed with baked apples, to Rowan who had only had a sandwich it was delicious. Skip enjoyed the left overs very much. Later Ginny picked up a torch and took Skip for a walk on the moor. To Rowan's surprise after one look at her for permission he went willingly enough as the door closed behind them Meg led Rowan to a small bedroom with twin beds. A pretty room with a wardrobe and washstand, chintz curtains and bedcovers, a lamp stood on the bedside table.

"This is where Janet and the children slept. Ginny sleeps here now but there's plenty of room for you but I'm afraid Skip will have to sleep in the kitchen, I hope he doesn't howl"

I don't think he will but thank you so much for not turning me away tonight."

We'll talk in the morning when we are fresh. Have a good night my dear. Ginny will be up presently" She went away to her room. Presently hearing Ginny come back with Skip, she went down to reassure him that she was still here. She settled him down on a blanket Ginny gave her. Ginny made up the fire in the range, put a guard around the sitting room fire and tidied up. Going upstairs they found themselves much too tired to chatter for long and soon fell asleep.

Chapter 17

A cockerel crowing woke Rowan as he shouted his message to the world. It was very dark. Looking at the little clock on the wash stand she could just make out that it was six o'clock. She smiled to herself remembering where she was; Meg's cottage. She wondered if Janet had woken here in the same way; that brought memories of Tom and her face clouded. She wished she had gone to him or that he was here. Her thoughts were interrupted as Ginny sat up and swung her feet to the floor.

"Good morning did you sleep well? I would rest a while if I were you. I must make the fire up. Meg won't stir for a bit when she does, I take her breakfast on a tray about half seven. You have a lie in, I'll take Skip out for you.

"Thank you but are you sure I can't help?"

"Not at the moment but maybe later on when you are rested you'll find your way around."

Rowan closed her eyes finding herself more tired than she realised. When she next surfaced there was hot water in the jug on the wash basin and a large tabby cat with green eyes was staring at her from the foot of the bed.

'Good morning to you too' the cat didn't even blink. Rowan washed and dressed in record time noting that it was now eight o'clock. She had not slept so late for a long time. Looking from the bedroom window she noted the garden was wild and neglected. Tom's stories of roses and millions of flowers were like a fairy tale, admitted it was late autumn but the garden was now mainly briars and dead stalks. Rose bushes still rambled everywhere badly in need of pruning, many plants were half buried in weeds. This garden hadn't had any loving for a long time.

Crossing to the little window on the landing Rowan saw that veg had been planted and gathered now the patch was left untidy and desolate, a few sprouts and cabbages still stood alone while fruit canes leant against wire posts that sagged drunkenly. There were no doves in the dove cot.

She ran down to the kitchen to find Meg sitting in the rocker a grey cat curled in her lap.

"Good morning Maid" The clear eyes locked onto hers." I've risen early to see who blew in last night. Now I can see you are far prettier in morning light. I trust you slept well?"

"I did, thank you taking me in." The lavender eyes regarded her steadily.

"Any friend of the Penry's is always welcome. I was real fond of all of them. I get letters from Janet. Amy can't be bothered to write only at Christmas but then she has her hands full with her brood. Tell me how they are all getting on. How is Tom really, poor boy?"

As Rowan ate she told Meg all that had happened. She listed carefully then sat back in her chair eyes closed. Rowan thought she had fallen asleep again and quietly rose and washed her dishes in the sink, not knowing where to put them she returned them to the table just as Ginny came in with Skip.

"Here she is, silly dog, she hasn't left you." Skip threw himself at Rowan whining as she fondled him. Ginny poured herself a cup of tea. "He didn't want to come with me this morning for a while then he kept pestering to come back; he knew where you were. He's very loyal but then collies are. My Dad's got two and Barry my fiancé has three, wonderful dogs. Anyway I must get on, now you have company Auntie, I am going across to the farm. The chickens have been fed and Clover, she's the pony by the way Rowan and there is a pig too. They are all done. I must give some thought to my wedding. We are getting married after Christmas so lots to do. I will see you later. Have a good gossip. There is ham cheese and tomatoes in the pantry and a slab of my Mother's fruit cake. I'll be back to see to dinner. Bye"

"Always in a hurry Ginny but she is a good girl. She is marrying a young farmer in January, going to live on his farm about five miles from here. I shall not see her so often then. Her parents John and Helen Mclean have a farm just down the road from here so she is able to stay with me. I need someone here now, I have no relatives apart from my sister and her two boys but she is not well and her husband died last year. That is where I intended Janet and her family to go but fate intervened as it does." She thought for a moment before continuing. "Do you have any plans other than to wait for Tom to make his mind up? He must heal before he commits himself so he is best left to it until he's ready. Tell me about yourself what you did while growing up."

Rowan told her about her parents and baby Ned, how her Aunt Jean was moving to be with her sister so Rowan was not needed so much now. Last night she had told Meg about her father and Bill Wilkins but she explained everything again also how she spent her days at the vets and the illustrations she did for Ralph Conway the writer, also about her love nature and her little dispensary with all the animals she had cared for.

"Well now, shall we have a cup of tea before I tell you my story?" Meg rose to put the kettle on but Rowan jumped up.

"Let me. You stay there, I can do it. I can cook you know, Mother taught me. I was not altogether a wild child of the woods." She laughed. Meg thought how nice a girl she was and made up her mind. After Rowan had laid a light lunch on small table so they could sit by the fire, cleared away after they had eaten then taken Skip for a short run, Meg resumed her talk.

"I used to be very fit when the Penry's were here but over the years my strength started to slip away. I had a bad fall two years back followed by pneumonia and was never well after, that's when Ginny came to look after me. She needed a job, her parents are my friends so it suited, then she met Barry Jenkins and I knew I wouldn't have her for long. I don't like being looked after by strangers so I was a bit worried. Now I may have found the answer. Would you like to stay while you wait for Tom?" Her eyes twinkled. "I believe you are in love with him, maybe him with you?"

"I don't know, sometimes his letters are quite loving, other times they seem just friendly. I do believe that he cares for me but he is very mixed up. He seems to be getting better working with Matt he loves working with animals and says Matt is teaching him a lot."

"Good you seem very well suited but you must have patience for him to come to you and I'm sure that he will. Now what do you say to taking Ginny's place for a while. I can pay you a small wage and your keep. If you can take some eggs to market or any produce that we have surplus, you can have money from that for your bottom draw. I have a good income. My husband left me comfortably off. He had several investments which I don't understand but my solicitor and my bank manager take care of all that. This cottage is mine and they assure me all is in order so I can afford to have someone care for me. Do you want to check with your parents first?"

Rowan clasped her hands with delight. "I would love to take care of you and this lovely little cottage. I will my parents of course but not where I am not yet or Bill or my Father will be over here so if it's alright with you and you are certain that's what you want I will write to my mother. May I tell Tom what I'll be doing?"

"Of course tell him I would love to see him again. He said he was going to take care of me when I was old he was only about eleven or twelve, I remember.

"Thank you so much." Rowan hugged her. "You make me feel I have a purpose in life again without pressure."

"I hope you will do these illustrations for your writer friend, maybe you could sell some in town. You are very good. Isn't it exciting?"

Rowan was beginning to feel excited. "There's a thought." She hesitated. "Will Ginny mind that I take her job? I would hate to upset her."

"We'll ask her when she comes in. I think she will be glad as she has a lot on at the moment with getting married and moving at the same time."

Ginny had been worrying about Meg for some time and was delighted to be told that Rowan was taking over. They chattered dinner, delighted that a suitable solution had been found. Rowan fell asleep that night feeling that she had come home.

Chapter 18

Christmas was bright but very cold. Bitter winds swept the country with sudden flurries of snow. Trees were blown down blocking roads and sadly reminding Tom of Ruth's tragic death. However he enjoyed working with Matt who was a good patient teacher who never grew tired of explaining. Tom had improved in health a lot. He was calmer in himself only occasionally the nightmares would return and he would wake the household with screams of terror before sobbing himself back to sleep. The first time this happened Janet was petrified and scared for the children but Matt reassured her.

"Don't worry the boys sleep very soundly and Tom's room is the other side of the house. I have explained that Tom sometimes has nightmares and not to be afraid as we go to him and calm him so they seem not bothered."

"Thank Goodness but I wish we could help him."

"Only time and security will do that. I think there's a big improvement already at least he can face people now and is getting better with that every day."

Tom found tending animals soothing and wished that he could do more. Matt sent him out on small jobs that he knew he could cope with and in the evening sat with him with veterinary books and diagrams, set him simple examinations and tests all of which Tom absorbed like s sponge. Matt declared to Janet that Tom would make a great vet nurse if it were possible for him to go to a college for a bit. Tom had problems with reading and writing as his schooling had been almost nothing but he was very grateful to Geoffrey Arlington who had spend so much time with him when he was courting Janet back in Blackberry cottage through the winter months. Although Geoffrey had broken Janet's heart in the end by marrying someone else and asking her to only be his mistress (an offer she had turned down immediately) he had spent long winter evenings with Tom bringing books on gardening and fishing, Tom being a very sharp boy had taken to reading and was often seen in winter evenings with a book. These sessions had helped him considerably and with Janet's help during his teens he was almost up to standard. Now Matt had taken over all this, Tom was very happy to take in all he could. He would have loved to be able to go to college for a while but his unstable state and lack of money made this impossible so he made the most of this opportunity to learn all he could from Matt.

Tom thought a lot about Rowan and found that he missed her company more than he thought he would. He began remembering their walks and talks in the woods, then found he was picturing more the way her elfin face lit up when she was happy, the way her thick chestnut hair caught the sunlight when it slipped its pins tumbling over her shoulders, the way her tawny eyes lit up when she was startled. More and more these images teased his senses and he found himself missing her. He wrote occasionally and found the need to write more often, telling her what he was doing and promising to come to see her at Meg's cottage as soon as he could. He so wanted to see Meg again too. Rowan wrote back, the bond growing all the while.

She wrote just after Christmas to tell him about her new job, her excitement filing her letter. She told how she had visited a gift shop in town and they had agreed on seeing her work to take several of her illustrations, frame them and sell them in their small art gallery so she had purchased an easel to make it easier to paint anywhere she wanted rather than using the kitchen table in everyone's way. She had met Ginny's parents the Mcleans and liked them very much. Best of all she had been in the garden feeding the hens when a loud honking noise made her jump, on hearing a whirring of wings she looked up to a sight she could never have imagined, hundreds of wild geese flew in a large v shape flew overhead their leader hooting instructions all the while. They flew so low Rowan could see the marking on their wings and their outstretched necks, there were so many they filled the sky and seemed to take forever to pass. She had ran to the house to ask where they had come from and where were they going? Meg told her they were Wild Geese who crossed from breeding grounds to feeding grounds at certain times of the year, although she said she had never seen them so far south as this. Rowan was so thrilled she looked for them every day and enclosed a sketch for Tom to keep. She ended her letter with love from Rowan which made his heart leap. He began to believe he may be falling in love.

Tom rarely saw Amy. Her way of life was too busy and noisy the few times he stayed with she had little time to talk, the young ones claiming her attention. He liked Sep very much and they always had a beer and a good chat when they met. It was to Joe and Tilly he turned when he needed someone to talk other than Janet. Their house would always be home to him as he had spent his time with them when Janet had moved to the shop and Amy had married Sep. It was from their cottage he had left to go to war. They always showed him that he was loved and wanted since he was a lad. He never went back to the cottage but once to collect his things. The memories of Ruth were too strong there and he could not pass the spot without feeling of deep regret and sadness. He blamed himself more than anyone knew. However memories of life in the cottage itself were happy ones and he often thought about their blackberry picking days when he worked with the charcoal burners and Janet sold her homemade cakes and pies to keep them all in food and clothes. His love and admiration for his older sister were unbounded. She had cared for them since their parents died and she and Amy had gone to work at Bratton Court where Amy had been cruelly treated by the housekeeper there, wrongly accused of theft and beaten senseless. He himself had to go to a local farmer to work although only eight. The farmer had told Janet he would send him to school with his boys in return for some work on the farm, this never materialised he too was beaten and abused by the farmers sons. Janet had taken them away and cared for them like a mother until they were taken in by Meg who found work on her sister's farm which they never reached. They came on the cottage in the forest by accident and lived quite happily there for several years.

Peter, Tom's son now flourished under Janet's care. He got on well with James and Dan and looked forward to going to school with them but was yet to his dismay too young and could only enjoy the evenings when Janet put him at the table to learn to read and write. He adored his father following him around. When he could, Tom made time for him, played with him and helped him to adjust, of his mother he spoke not at all after the first couple of weeks. Most of the time Tom thought only of animals and their problems, working with Matt, studying at night and bonding with his son kept him fully occupied. When he had time to think his thoughts more and more turned to Rowan. He longed to go to her but realised that he must heal himself and be able to work to support her if anything was to come of these feelings. He knew that she was safe with Meg and he would get there one day if she still would want him that is. He dare not ask at the moment, he could only pray that she didn't meet anyone else in the meantime.

Chapter 19

Ginny's wedding took place January 15th. It was cold and frosty, everywhere glittered like Christmas. It was a pretty scene the trees stood white like brides themselves, it seemed the whole world was dressed just for her, grass crunched underfoot and the bay horses that drew her carriage blew plumes of steam from their nostrils, tossing their heads while champing at their bits. They were decorated with white plumes and ribbons and pulled a white carriage decked with garlands of greenery and pink roses. Ginny's parents had spared no expense. They had even sent a carriage for Rowan and Meg who although not feeling well insisted in going. Dressed in a lavender dress and coat with a grey fur hat, gloves and muff was every inch the lady. Rowan worried as she had few clothes with her, none of which were suitable for a wedding but Meg had sent her into town a few days before and she came back with a green wool dress and jacket which lit up her eyes and brought out the glints in her tawny hair which she wore loose curling down her back with a little nonsense hat completing her outfit.

The Norman church stood apart from the village, its square towers almost hidden in trees. It was very cold inside in spite of the huge stove that complete with guard stood at the back. Rowan was intrigued at the wall paintings and old tombs which lined the outer aisles she decided she would come back one day and source the history of this lovely building. There were too many people now piling in to the church to take in anything else. The scent of candles and flowers filled the church and music came softly from the hidden organ. Tawny Chrysanthemums and Ivy filled the windows, with russet and gold ribbons tying white ones to the ends of the pews, their perfume mingling with that of the candles. Meg and Rowan were lucky enough to find a seat not far from the front so had a good view of the proceedings. The bridegroom stood with his man looking decidedly nervous. He was a handsome man, tall and thickest with a shock of blond hair; his best man looked very much like him. Rowan deduced they were brothers.

The organ playing the wedding march heralded the arrival of the bride. When she entered, the congregation stood up and there was a gasp of delight. Ginny wore a white velvet gown, a white fur cape and carried a sheaf of red roses. The three bridesmaids, one of which was very tiny were dressed in red velvet and carried baskets of white roses and trailing fern. On her father's arm she glided down the aisle radiant to meet her groom who greeted her with a smile. The service was not over long and to the joyous peel of bells they emerged into the frosty sunlight in a shower of confetti and rice. The reception was held at a local inn 'The Green Man' so old it seemed to be growing from the ground and had grown its own thatch. It was very difficult to see what the inside was like as it was so crowded. The meal was lavish and delicious, champagne flowed freely. Rowan enjoyed it all very much but just before speeches Meg felt unwell, she had eaten and drunk very little. The carriage was sent for and Rowan and a relative of the Mcleans helped her in to a score of commiserations from people who knew her well. Rowan was worried that it had all been too much for her. Once back at the cottage Rowan made up the fire and helped Meg to bed with a hot water bottle and a cup of tea after which she fell asleep and Rowan was able to take Skip out and feed the animals. She realised that Meg was very fragile and must be taken great care of. She also realised for the first time that she would have to stay whatever happened between her nad Tom as long as Meg needed her.

Meg was much better the following day but Rowan persuaded her to spend a day or two in bed, making up the fire in her room and bringing some tasty food to tempt her. Meg protested at first but gave in rather too easily Rowan thought and she worried, as Meg refused to have the doctor so all she could do was to keep her warm and let her rest. On the third day she insisted on getting up to sit in the parlour with her cats. Just as Rowan got her settled there was a knock on the door which she opened to find Helen Mclean with a large bunch of flowers and a basket on her arm.

"Hello Rowan. How is Meg? Are you coping alright? I wanted to come down before but with Ginny moving straight after the wedding and going on honeymoon tomorrow it's been a busy week."

"Do come in Mrs Mclean, I'm sure she will be very pleased to see you, she is feeling better but a bit miserable because she isn't able to do anything. She is in the sitting room. Go through and I will bring some tea."

"She is so lucky to have you since Ginny had to leave, I honestly don't know what we would have done if you hadn't been here." Helen handed Rowan the basket. "Just a few goodies to tempt her appetite and some flowers left from the wedding." She went through to Meg and the exclamations of delight from Meg were rewarding. Rowan took through a tray of tea and biscuits before closing the door and taking the opportunity to take Skip for a long walk. Helen was leaving just as she got back. She gave Rowan a hug and again said how pleased she was that Meg was so well looked after and that it was a worry off Ginny's mind as well.

"Don't be afraid to come for me if you need anything or Meg is ill, we are all here to help. Don't feel alone come up if you just want a chat anytime." With a cheery wave she set off back to the farm. The visit had been good for Meg. That evening she chattered like her old self and ate a good supper. Rowan felt much happier about her and treated herself by writing long letters to Tom and her mother. She would have loved to receive one from her but felt she dare not yet give her address.

Chapter 20

It was a hard winter, the kind that starts at the beginning of January and lasts until the end of April. The daffodils were buried in snow and the bluebells didn't appear at all until late May, when they finally made their appearance spring was full on. Trees quickly clothed themselves in green leaves birds were mad with song and rushing to build nests. The wild geese flew every day between their feeding ground and their resting place. Rowan was never tired of seeing them and would rush outside or to a window to try to count them as they filled the sky overhead. She wished she could fly back and fore like them so that she could go to Tom then come back to nurse Meg. Primroses and violets bloomed under the hedges, cowslips gave off their powerful scent and she picked little bunches for Meg's room. As the snow disappeared altogether the garden became alive with masses of spring bulbs and the promise of much more to come. Rowan took over the garden between looking after Meg. She would help her down in the mornings after she cleaned up and lit the fires to warm the rooms. They would breakfast together then Rowan would feed the pig, chickens and cats see to Clover then take Skip for a walk. Ginny's parents were regular visitors to Meg so during their visits Rowan would catch the bus to town where she ordered the delivery of groceries and animal feed stuffs, do the shopping for herself and Meg also taking the opportunity of placing her sketches in the little gallery where to her surprise they began to sell slowly at first then as visitors came around rather more quickly. Rowan loved the garden and dreamt that should Tom come it might be restored to some of its former glory. While Meg was resting in the afternoons was the best time. She consulted with Meg and followed the patterns laid out by the roses and the windling paths not really knowing what she was doing, she studied gardening books at night questioning Meg about the pruning and kept a weed fir burning day and night.

Soon the strawberries were in flower, May blossom filled the air and many buds and flowers she did not know began to open, freed of their many weeds they seemed determined to show off many blossoms and the garden began to take shape. Rowan was lost when it came to the vegetable patch but John Mclean took pity on her sending one of his retired farm hands a man named Albert Penrose to sort it out for her. He proved a treasure, bent back and bandy legged, his white hair firmly held in place with an ancient cap which John whispered to Rowan 'he had never seen off his head all the years that he worked for him and he firmly believed it was the same one as well' Rowan giggled at this but soon saw what he meant. Albert's toothless grin did her heart good as he soon converted the depressing vegetable patch into a neat patch of soil with long rows of peas, beans, parsnips, carrots, swedes, cabbages and everything else he could think of, even better he helped trim the overgrown hedges and trees. Rowan couldn't imagine managing without him.

The Mcleans agreed that Alfred should stay and he became permanent addition to the welfare of the cottage, arriving at nine o'clock and departing at four thirty precisely. He later confessed to Rowan that' It got him out from under the missus feet and gave him sommat to do'. The garden was a haven for birds and butterflies which gave Rowan plenty to sketch and paint. Soon honeysuckle and wild roses climbed as they used to through the hedges and over the cottage, mad blackbirds scolded and fretted about their babies although the cats never turned a hair and appeared bored with the whole bird thing preferring to sit on Megs lap or sprawl out in the sun also now ignoring Skip altogether and he them. House martins built above bedroom windows and woke everyone with their sweet cheeping every morning. Skip chased young rabbits in the meadow, never lucky enough to catch one.

The raspberries flowered and formed their delicious fruit. From her chair Meg coached Rowan into the art of jam making, unable to do those things she had always loved to do, she delighted in teaching Rowan and the two spent many happy mornings trying new methods with all the fruit and veg. Albert was often sent home with jars and dishes for' Susan to try'. By August Meg began to fail suddenly it seemed she was unable to manage the stairs and her bed had to be brought down to the sitting room where a fire had to be kept burning day and night. A local lad brought coal and logs once a week and Rowan was kept busy with this. A bell was placed by the bed so if anything was needed in the night Rowan could be there in an instant. Although she wrote often she had no word from Tom in over a month and she fretted. The wild geese flying over now seemed to have a mournful call and she no longer ran to see them.

The long hot summer seemed to be pulling in early. Rowan under Meg's instructions and the many recipe books in the kitchen made pickles, chutneys and preserves, saved eggs in isinglass for the winter when the hens would stop laying. She preserved all she could of fruit and vegetables and to her surprise had much success. She was very pleased when Meg praised her but Meg herself was fading. Ginny and her husband came to see her, later Ginny came out into the garden to Rowan and cried.

"She's not going to last much longer, Rowan. I'm so glad you are here for her. Mother warned me she was not good but I haven't been able to come until now. I'm pregnant and haven't been well. Aunty Meg was so thrilled when we told her just now but I can't bear it." She sobbed on Rowan's shoulder Barry came out of the cottage and took his wife in his arms.

"Come away home now, love. Rowan is here to look after her and your mum is nearby, they will let us know how she does. You must not get too upset at this stage." They said goodbye to Meg, Ginny hugging Rowan and they left.

John and Helen came to sit one night with Meg, Helen had tears in her eyes as she left. "Come and fetch me dear if anything happens, day or night. I will be expecting you." She patted Rowan's arm and turned back to say good night to Meg.

Rowan felt alone and apprehensive, she had never nursed anyone before least of all at the end of their life. She was fearful of not doing the right thing. She sat in the kitchen and sobbed for Tom and Meg and wished that her mother was here. If she wasn't so fearful of Bill Wilkins she would have risked sending for her mother or aunt but being here alone made her more nervous than ever of him finding her.

Meg lingered on. September crept in with misty mornings and cool nights. The smell of Albert's bonfires grew stronger and mushrooms appeared in the dewy meadow. She fed Meg mushroom soup and chicken soup which Meg enjoyed and seemed to grow a little stronger. One day in late September when the doctor had been, they had made Meg more comfortable and he had left a potion to ease her pain and to help her sleep although she seemed to Rowan to slip frequently in and out of sleep whether it was day or night. Rowan found the house too confining and after checking her patient stepped out into the garden. She sat on the long bench under Meg's window with Skip lying on her feet. The scent of night stocks and Chrysanths mingled with the smell of burning leaves. The evenings were growing colder and brilliant colour was creeping into the trees. Rowan pulled her coat around her wondering where she would go when Meg finally passed on. She was alone now and more than a little afraid. She had saved some money but where would she live that wouldn't prove too expensive? She would have to get a job of some kind although at the moment she felt too tired and dispirited to even consider it. She couldn't go home, more and more gloomy thoughts chased through her tired brain, what would she do with Skip when she was out at work? It was so perfect here, everything had slotted into place but it wouldn't be easy to find anything like it anywhere else. She had grown to love Meg, the garden and animals. Who would care for them? Her sad thoughts were interrupted by the sound of someone walking briskly down the lane beside her, the sound of men's boots. Skip gave a low warning growl. Rowan quickly slipped indoors with the dog, locking the doors. The gate squeaked, afraid to look through the window she waited until there was a sharp knock on the door.

"Who is it?" she called over Skip barking, her voice trembling in spite of herself. It was someone strange she knew by Skip's reaction and her own senses.

"Don't be afraid, Rowan. It's me Tom." Both she and Skip recognized his voice at once. Skip stopped barking and started to wag his tail. Rowan flung open the door and in an instant his arms were around her. Time stood still as he kissed here with the passion he had wanted to bring her all summer. Skip danced around now with a different sort of barking.

"Oh! Tom I can't believe it. I wanted you to come so much."

"Yes my sweetheart and I'll not be going anywhere unless you send me away. What on earth's that?"

The Geese filled the darkening skies, hooting as they came, there seemed to be more than ever and they flew low. Rowan and Tom could almost feel the beating of their wings as the great birds made their long journey to their winter quarters. There were hundreds and they took their time to pass, after they were gone they left a great silence and an empty sky.

"Rowan was in tears." The wild Geese are going home for the winter as you have come home. They will be back they always come back.

"So will I my little fawm. I love you Rowan I didn't realize how much until we were apart so long. Can you love me?"

"I do I always have. Come in to Meg; let's shut the door and please kiss me"

So he did.

Chapter 21

Meg rallied enough in the morning to meet Tom. Surprisingly bright for once, she hugged and kissed him.

"Well my boy, come at last. You have grown a bit but I can see you have had a bad time. Who would have thought it all those years ago?" My little lad who used to chop the wood and come to look after me now I'm old as you said you would. Look at you now."

"Not so little now" Tom had tears in his eyes as he gently embraced her. "To be honest Meg you don't look much different to how I remember you."

"Flattery will get you everywhere young man." Meg was almost coquettish. Her strange lavender coloured eyes though faded were very bright. "But you have changed a lot." She looked with delight at the tall young man before her. Although his hair was no longer the bright gold it had been and was streaked with grey his eyes were still the bright blue she remembered. His face was rather lined for so young a man but he was still very handsome and the smile as sweet as ever. Rowan found it hard to relate her man of the woods with the carefree lad she saw before her now. It was almost as if he had shed a skin an emerged a new creature, true his eyes still held a strange look of sadness when in repose but the quick smile on the beautiful mouth came more readily and his face was light and open.

"Yes I remember telling you I would look after you."

"You did Boy and I've waited for you. I knew you would come I told my little Rowan so, she has been a good girl, Take care of each other, my darlings"

The once sharp eyes were fading and soon she was asleep again. Tom wiped a tear from his eye.

"She was so good to us when we needed someone desperately, we didn't want to leave her and I never thought I would come back here."

After supper when the animals were fed and Tom had met Albert, admired the garden and taken Skip for his walk he and Rowan sat holding hands and talked, Skip snoring between their feet not willing to leave either of them. The cats had retired to be with Meg as she slept and the house was quiet. It was a time for talking, whispers and promises. Rowan came alive in his arms, when his kisses deepened she wanted more, when he held her close she wanted closer, when his hands found her breasts she wanted his mouth; all the hatred and fear of Bill Wilkins touching of her vanished under a wave of love and desire. Tom was gentle with her as one would be with a shy woodland creature. He desired her but let her lead, wanted her but let her want more. Their union was gentle and beautiful growing in passion as she trusted him and gave her all. He accepted with gratitude and love and gave all of himself without fear that she wouldn't return the love he gave so gladly. To them both it was the coming together of two who had no reason to trust but did gladly and knew it was right knowing it was their time.

Skip howling at the door startled them awake, the fire had burned itself out and the room was cold. Wrapped in each other's arms they had not been conscious of it but now Rowan woke startled and cold. She rushed into Meg's room realising there had been no summons in the night. Rowan stopped hand to mouth as she saw Meg had slipped away in the night a smile on her face, the lovely lavender eyes closed as in sleep. Tom took her in his arms as she cried for her friend, tears in his own eyes.

"Don't fret my darling, it's how she would have wanted and there was no better way for her or for you."

"I know but I wanted to be with her at the end but I didn't know it would be so soon. I'm so glad you came in time she was so pleased to see you and to know how we felt about each other. She seemed to know that we were right for each other. We must go to the farm and tell them but what are we to do? We must leave here soon, where can we go?"

"Don't worry little one, I'll take care of you. We'll go home to get married first then the world is ours. We'll find somewhere."

"I'll be sorry to leave here it feels like home now. But my home is where you are. We'll find our home somewhere."

Tom left for the farm while Rowan saw to the animals who never cared for anyone's sorrow as long as they were fed and watered as usual except for Skip who sensing her distress kept very close but didn't want his breakfast. Helen came back with Tom and the doctor arrived soon after. Helen lovingly laid Meg out in her best satin nightgown and fetched greenery from the garden. Tom stood with tears in his eyes for he could see in the peaceful face the kind woman who had taken them all in and card for him and his sisters and now his beloved Rowan. Tom ran essential errands for everyone while Ginny came to stay and help Rowan.

The last day of September was a clear warm autumn day with a misty morning followed by sunshine and a light breeze which blew bronze and gold leaves like confetti across the mourners and the coffin as they walked the churchyard. The lovely old church was warm and scented with flowers, Michaelmas daisies and the gold and tawny Chrysanthemums that Meg had loved so much. People came from miles around for Meg, who had lived here for many years and helped many with different needs. The service was moving and sincere, soon over and Margaret Lucinda Thornton was laid to rest in the churchyard where her husband and son were waiting among flowers in softly blowing grass and the murmur of ancient trees above her.

Tom decided then and there he would buy the headstone and the grave would always be attended. Janet and Amy came and were upset that they had not visited her when she was alive, they stayed a couple of days with Rowan although cross with her that she hadn't told them where she was and begged her to come home with Tom. John Mclean invited Tom to stay at the farm and he was pleased to do so for Rowan's sake. He came every day to see the girls and help Albert who wondered how long he would be needed. No one knew what Meg had put in her will so no one could say. Her solicitor had been summoned back in the summer so patience was needed. Rowan assumed the cottage would be left to Ginny who came back when Janet and Amy left as there were things to be cleared and sorted. Rowan mentally prepared to leave as soon as the cottage was cleared and the will was read. It was about a week later that a letter arrived from Meg's solicitors. They would call on Monday of the following week to read the will. They requested the presence of Miss Rowena Berryman, Mrs Virginia Jenkins, Mr and Mrs Mclean and the Penry's. Rowan was surprised that she should be asked maybe Meg in her kindness of heart had left her a small token. It would be wonderful if she had.

Mr Pearce of Pearce and Makepeace arrived very punctually at eleven o'clock a tall thin man with grey hair and a black moustache which made him look very odd indeed. Rowan and Ginny who had arrived the night before were hard put to keep from giggling at their first sight of him. Tom came down with the Mcleans but neither Amy nor Janet were able to travel again so soon and sent their apologies. Mr Pearce was a sombre silent man who as soon as coffee was served and everyone else present opened his briefcase.

Clearing his throat he began a list of formalities which everyone waited with impatience for him to finish. Finally he began the bequests. Meg had remembered many friends and neighbours with small gifts and bequests even including Alfred giving him her late husband's watch and five pounds. To her sister Hetty and her two sons she had left one hundred pounds and a small bundle of shares. To John Mclean she had left her late husband's books, his collection of pipes, medals and maps which were John's passion as well and he was delighted to receive. To Helen she had left items of jewellery and her figurines. To Ginny the sum of five hundred pounds and a couple of small items of furniture for her new home (at which Ginny burst into tears). Next came the Penry's, to Janet and Amy fifty pounds each, to Tom five hundred. The solicitor paused; everyone waited with bated breath, what about the cottage? Clearing his throat and taking a few sips of water, Mr Pearce continued. "To Miss Rowan Berryman my cottage and all contents there in, (excluding bequests) the grounds around, livestock and chattels and the remainder of my estate in the hope she finds happiness and contentment with her future husband in the place where I spent the happiest years of my life." There was a stunned silence for a moment as the solicitor finished speaking and began to sort his papers. Rowan sat in total shock believing she was in a dream until Tom's arms came around her. "There's the answer to your questions, my love." Ginny gave a scream of delight and flung her arms around both of them as far as her bump would allow.

"I'm so thrilled for you. Meg thought the world of you and it couldn't go to a better person. You'll be safe now with Tom."

"I don't know about that, she may not want me to share her cottage." Tom teased. "I'm sure that's not the case."John Mclean came to shake her hand and Helen to kiss her. "We are delighted for you and to keep you as our neighbour. Do please come and see us at any time."

"Mr Pearce is going now" Ginny called. "He can't stay for lunch he has other business waiting." With a tremendous effort Rowan forced herself to concentrate, going up to the solicitor she shook his outstretched hand. "Thank you for all your attentions and for taking care of Meg all these years."

"It was a pleasure, my dear. She was a very sweet lady and I hope you will be very happy here. If there is anything we can do for you just let me know." Rowan thanked him again and promised to call him in a few weeks to settle her affairs. As the Mcleans left declining lunch as they were taking Ginny home, they hugged her and wished her well. Tom was to stay with them until he and Rowan returned to Indian Queens to be married.

Rowan was still unable to take in her windfall. She questioned Tom. "Do you think if I hadn't come along she would have left more to Ginny?"

"Who can say Rowan? She made up her mind that you deserved it and you should be grateful. Meg would only do what Meg wanted to do and it gave her enormous pleasure to repay you for the kindness you showed her while you repaid her for the kindness she showed you. Things work like that sometimes. I think it's wonderful and I'm so happy for you."

"We are so lucky Tom to be able to stay here and enjoy what we both love so much"

"To find a haven like this after all the suffering is unbelievable." Tom's face clouded for a moment then his merry laugh rang out as he spotted Skip chasing around the field like a deer after a rabbit he had no hope of catching.

"I know I am being silly. What are we going to do now? I am still overwhelmed by it all." Tom picked her up and swung her around.

"First we are going to ask the Mcleans to mind the place while we go home to get married. Then after a week's honeymoon somewhere nice we are coming back to live happy ever after. I am going to see if I can enrol for veterinary classes and maybe find some work in a surgery somewhere. It may be I'll be a way part of the week will you mind? You my darling should develop those lovely art pictures you do and open a small gallery if only in the summer." Rowan's face lit up. "What a lovely idea. You do get some good ideas. Let's go and do it."

Chapter 22

They returned to Indian Queens for a Christmas wedding. Rowan was in trepidation about meeting her parents but she was welcomed with open arms. Her mother and aunt wept as they hugged her while little Ned demanded to be told 'Wose dat? Mama wose dat?' "Don't you remember your big sister?" Rowan swung him around until he giggled. A while later he went around everyone stating with pointing finger. 'Dat Rown dat is'. He was a delight, fat and round as a robin with a dark tuft of hair and big hazel eyes, an infectious chuckle which showed off his new teeth which came through according to his Aunt Jean 'faster than we can cope with them' climbing everywhere he could reach. Rowan sighed when she thought of how much of his babyhood she had missed. Worried about meeting her father she was delighted when he came in to be swept into his arms and hugged soundly.

"Thought you'd sneak back did yer? Think yer old dad is goin ter pay for a fancy wedding, did yer?"

"Of course I didn't. I can pay for my own now."

"Oh! High and mighty, Miss." But her father was grinning from ear to ear. "We'll say no more about that. Now this young man has some explaining to do." Jed shook Tom's hand vigorously, "Joe told me your story lad, I'm right sorry for all you've been through. I know yer don't want to talk about it but I'm right proud ter have yer as a son."

Dora hugged him. "Welcome back Tom. I'm so pleased for you both and I know you will look after her. Your sisters must be very proud of you too. Now we have a wedding to plan."

Janet and Amy were indeed proud of the outcome after so much tragedy, overcome with their inheritance that Meg should have thought so much of them. Janet pleased that she had kept in touch (Amy more than a little guilty that she hadn't). Thrilled that Tom and Rowan were getting wed at Christmas they urged Rowan out on a shopping expedition, not once but several times, Sep warning Amy not to buy expensive things unless he was with her to which instruction she paid very little heed.

Joe and Tilly were delighted to see them and hear their news. Rowan was quite over come to receive as wedding present from them a complete bone china dinner and tea service decorated with wild flowers.

Tom walked with Rowan through the churchyard to place flowers and holly on Ruth's grave. "What about Peter, Tom. Have you told him about us?"

"I thought we should go down both of us and tell him together. We'll go tomorrow if it's alright with you. He's quite happy with Janet but I want him to live with us and have a settled home, don't you agree?"

"Yes very much, I think he has been put about enough, it's time that he had a real home again." They wandered back in the frosty night unaware of the cold so deep were they in plans for the future.

They travelled to Janet's the next day. Peter was wild with delight to see his father and to Rowan's surprise pleased to see her too asking endless questions about Skip and the animals he had seen in her dispensary. She had to explain where they had all gone. When Tom told him that he would be coming to live with them in a little while, the first questions he asked were, would Skip be there and could he have some rabbits and a shed like Rowan's to look after them in?" On being told he could and there were many chickens, cats, a pig and a pony, he couldn't see why he couldn't come right away.

Janet laughed when they told her. "He's a lovely little boy, never complains, very placid. I think my boys are a bit too old for him they always want to do things he can't, although Dan's only six he's in school with James now and thinks Peter is a baby. It will be good for him to have a home of his own.

The evening flew by, Tom playing with his son until bedtime when Matt came home and they fell into their usual veterinary discussions. Janet carried Rowan off to put the boys to bed after which they talked weddings.

Before they returned to the Berryman's, Tom took Rowan into town to buy her engagement and wedding ring. She chose an emerald, because it reminded her of the woods, also a plain gold wedding band. As she had asked Emily Treggorran to be her bridesmaid and Violet and Cissie to be her flower girls, she bought them small lockets as wedding favours, buying Tom cuff links as her gift to him as he bought her pearls. Well satisfied with their purchases she left Tom to buy his suit. Joe was to be his groomsman but as he said. "My suit has only seen two weddings and three funerals so I won't need a new one."

A week before Christmas it snowed, a light dusting enough to make everything festive, Christmas fell on a Sunday, so they planned the wedding for Christmas Eve, '(so we can have a magical weekend)' Rowan declared.

It was a special time. The morning of the wedding dawned cold but bright the snow a fairy tale background. Rowan had chosen an ivory gown with her veil held in place with a circle of mistletoe. Emily, a beautiful redhead wore green with a circlet of Christmas roses while the little flower girls wore ivory like the bride and carried baskets of mistletoe and Christmas roses. The children were dressed in their very best winter coats and were too excited to stand still so it was to parent's great relief when the service over they could erupt out into the snow. Bells pealed all day first for the wedding then practice for Christmas services. Rowan was radiant, so excited she had tied red ribbons around Skip's collar to his great disgust and insisted that Aunt Jean brought him to the service where he slumped to the floor chin on paws and went to sleep. Jed had insisted on a reception at the Inn, as said no one would want to do that and cook Christmas dinner next day. There weren't many guests but those who were there were genuine friends or family and the merry making sounded as if there were many more. Janet had brought Peter with James and Dan and after the cake was cut, her and Matt had to leave to take their brood home as no one had enough room to put so many up. Throwing confetti as the light began to fade they drove off, Tom assuring Peter that at the end of the week he would be down to fetch him home.

Tom and Rowan stayed at the Berryman's for their wedding night, leaving next day for a few days in Plymouth to enjoy the bright lights before returning to their home. They collected Peter on their way and a delighted Skip.

Back home they found the cottage warm and cosy. Helen had lit the fires and filled the larder. A note on the table told them the beds were aired and a casserole in the pantry, she would see them the following afternoon. A large parcel stood on the table beside the note, wrapped in Christmas paper. Peter couldn't wait for them to open it so they did. It contained two beautiful crocheted bedspreads and a set of new saucepans from Ginny, Berry and the Mcleans but more important from Peter's point of view a set of farmyard animals with a horse and cart which with much chatter he took to bed and settled as if he had lived here all his life.

Tom took Rowan in his arms. "Home at last my Darling. Are you happy?"

"I'm more than happy. We are going to have a wonderful life here aren't we?"

"I will do all in my power to make it so. I can't promise that I won't have those awful nightmares occasionally although they have almost gone now I have you in my arms. We will have ups and downs as everyone does but we have each other and Peter and maybe a brother or sister will come for him."

"I hope so. We know that we have Meg's blessing and family and friends to visit us. We will make a life that's good and it's the start of a new year."

"Remember our Unicorn? Do you think he might have been one or were we being silly?"

"I don't know, stranger things have happened but I do know the wild Geese will be back."

Rowan kissed him and turned to look through the window. "Look Tom it's snowing harder than ever. Perhaps we'll be cut off."

"Good." Tom said taking her once more in his arms. "Let it snow."

About the Author

Louise June James was born in the county of Staines, Middlesex in October 1938 to middle aged parents who having raised their family almost eighteen years before, had to start all over again. The family moved to a cottage in the hills of South Wales during the war. Louise was educated at St Michael's convent, Abergavenny. English and Art were her favourite subjects.

Writing since the age of twelve- Louise was made South Wales Editor for the childrens' page of Health from Herbs magazine. Small articles and poems followed. Louise's childhood in a remote rural area stimulated a great imagination and a deep love of nature and the countryside.

Louise married a childhood sweetheart and worked at several jobs, mainly in dispatch and export offices. Her hobbies at that time were breeding and exhibiting German shepherd dogs, reading and painting. When the marriage failed in 1962 Louise concentrated on art, mainly oils, exhibiting and selling at a local gallery. She married again in 1964, farming with her husband in the Black Mountains. Louise has three grown up sons from this marriage and wrote her first book (not published). When the marriage failed in 198), Louise raised her teenage sons unaided. Managing a pub for four years, then taking a course in Management Extention Louise worked for a while as a marketing Consultant for the hotel trade. At this time her interest returned to writing poetry for pleasure and studying Astrology and the supernatural.

Louise married Bryan James in 1989. His struggle to overcome the effects of a brain haemorrage, moved her to write a book for all who have come close to death or suffer some form of disability although this book received favourable comments it was not published. Bryan and Louise moved to Sussex in 1989 and lived there for nine years, Louise working in the book department of W. H. Smith which stimulated her to write The Blackberry Pickers in her spare time, before it was completed Bryan was taken ill with Chronic Fatigue Syndrome and had to give up his job as farm Manager. They moved back to Hereford where Louise has been able to continue writing having several poems published and completing her book.

Lightning Source UK Ltd.
Milton Keynes UK
UKOW04f1956250615

254153UK00001B/15/P